January was just about ~~sleep when a sudden~~ **her consciousness.**

Her eyes flew open.

She knew that noise. It was the one made by her back door alarm.

Someone was trying to come in.

January immediately thought of the black sedan she had seen earlier. The same one she had seen driving around yesterday.

Bolting out of bed, she paused only long enough to grab her cell phone—not even her shoes. Moving as fast as she could, she flew into Maya's bedroom.

"C'mon, baby, we've got to go," she signed as quickly as she could.

Maya had barely opened her eyes. January wasn't sure she had even gotten her message across to the girl, but there was no time to stop and sign it again.

They needed to hide.

Now.

* * *

Colton 911: Chicago—Love and danger come alive in the Windy City...

* * *

Dear Reader,

Welcome to another saga surrounding the very prolific Colton family. This one is about the branch started by twin brothers who wound up marrying twin sisters. The brothers, Ernest and Alfred, went into the medical technology field, while their wives, Farrah and Fallon, became interior designers who opened their own company. Alfred and Farrah had three daughters, while Ernest and Fallon had two sons and a daughter. And unlike some warring clans, everyone in these two families was close.

This story is about the youngest of Alfred and Farrah's three daughters. January Colton is an extremely dedicated social worker who gets pulled into a homicide case involving a deaf five-year-old little girl, Maya. The detective in charge, Sean Stafford, takes it upon himself to guard January and Maya when it becomes evident that they are being stalked, most likely targeted for elimination, because of what Maya might have witnessed.

So come, read and return for more. I promise you won't be sorry.

As always, I want to thank you for picking up one of my books to read. And from the bottom of my heart, I wish you someone to love who loves you back.

All the best,

Marie Ferrarella

COLTON 911: THE SECRET NETWORK

Marie Ferrarella

HARLEQUIN

ROMANTIC SUSPENSE

Special thanks and acknowledgment are given to
Marie Ferrarella for her contribution to the
Colton 911: Chicago miniseries.

HARLEQUIN®
ROMANTIC
SUSPENSE™

Recycling programs
for this product may
not exist in your area.

ISBN-13: 978-1-335-62877-0

Colton 911: The Secret Network

Copyright © 2021 by Harlequin Books S.A.

This edition published by arrangement with Harlequin Books S.A.

For questions and comments about the quality of this book,
please contact us at CustomerService@Harlequin.com.

Harlequin Enterprises ULC
22 Adelaide St. West, 40th Floor
Toronto, Ontario M5H 4E3, Canada
www.Harlequin.com

Printed in U.S.A.

USA TODAY bestselling and RITA® Award–winning author **Marie Ferrarella** has written more than two hundred and fifty books for Harlequin, some under the name Marie Nicole. Her romances are beloved by fans worldwide. Visit her website, marieferrarella.com.

Books by Marie Ferrarella

Harlequin Romantic Suspense

Colton 911: Chicago

Colton 911: The Secret Network

The Coltons of Kansas

Exposing Colton Secrets

The Coltons of Mustang Valley

Colton Baby Conspiracy

Cavanaugh Justice

A Widow's Guilty Secret
Cavanaugh's Surrender
Cavanaugh Rules
Cavanaugh's Bodyguard
Cavanaugh Fortune
How to Seduce a Cavanaugh
Cavanaugh or Death
Cavanaugh Cold Case
Cavanaugh in the Rough
Cavanaugh on Call
Cavanaugh Encounter
Cavanaugh Vanguard
Cavanaugh Cowboy
Cavanaugh's Missing Person
Cavanaugh Stakeout
Cavanaugh in Plain Sight

Visit the Author Profile page at Harlequin.com for more titles.

This book is dedicated to

My Other Daughters.

To Sandra Lee,

Whom I have known

Since her first day of kindergarten,

And to Tiffany Melgar,

Whom I got to know when she was just a little older,

But no less wonderful.

And to my flesh-and-blood daughter, Jessica Ferrarella,

Who has never read a single one of my books,

But whom I love dearly anyway.

You make my heart smile, girls.

I'm so glad that you are all in my life.

With love,

Mama

Prologue

January Colton hurried across the restaurant's main dining area. By her watch, she was only five minutes late, but her sisters would make a big deal out of it since she was always running late. Usually just by a little bit, but never through her own fault. She just didn't have a job that could easily be wrapped up at day's end. Being a social worker just wasn't that sort of work.

"Sorry I'm late," she said to the two women who were already seated at the cozy round table.

Simone, the oldest sister and the only one of the three who had medium brown hair worn in a chin-length bob, raised her eyes to January's face. "Second verse, same as the first," she murmured with a patient smile.

"I'll have you know I was briefing the woman who's

going to be taking my place for the next couple of weeks," January informed her as she set down her bag.

Centering herself, she looked around the table. There was a plate of appetizers in the middle and three glasses of champagne, one by each of their place settings.

"Everything looks lovely, as always, Tatum," January, the tallest sister despite the fact that she was the youngest, said, complimenting the middle Colton sister. After all, the restaurant, True, was Tatum's baby. It had been for the last two years. The blonde, wavy haired Tatum had worked night and day to pull the farm-to-table restaurant together, turning it into the success it was today.

January's excuse was not lost on either of her siblings. "You actually have someone taking your place next week?" Simone asked.

"I do," January said proudly, picking up the menu and glancing at it.

"So this is really on the level?" Tatum questioned January. They were all workaholics, but of the three of them, January was the most notoriously dedicated. They had lost count of the vacations that had been planned and then hadn't materialized.

"Absolutely," January replied.

They had made plans for this joint getaway, booking a flight as well as reservations at a spa, but Simone was still skeptical about its taking place. "You're really going to do this?"

"Yes," January answered with emphasis. "I'm really going to do this."

Simone pinned their baby sister with a look. "You're not going to back out at the last minute?"

January frowned. "No."

"Or say that something 'just came up'?" Tatum pressed the issue, knowing that those were excuses that January had used to beg off before.

Exasperated, January put down her menu and looked from one of her sisters to the other. "What is it going to take to convince you two that I am really going to go on this way overdue spa vacation with you?"

"Way, *way* overdue," Tatum pointedly emphasized.

"Give it a rest, Tatum," January requested. "Now, what is it going to take to get the two of you to drop this and just move on?"

"You could try signing a statement in blood," Simone, a psychology professor with a PhD from the University of Chicago, suggested with an innocent smile. "We all know how quickly you can change your mind."

"Very funny coming from someone who just broke up with yet another lame guy," January commented, deciding to go on the offensive for a change. "Tell me, did you minor in having notoriously bad taste in men, or is that something that just comes naturally to you?"

The dark-haired thirty-two-year-old professor drew her shoulders back. "At least I'm trying, which is more than I can say for you."

January decided to retreat. She wasn't here to fight, she was here to mark the beginning of their mutually anticipated holiday.

But she did want to make a point.

"There aren't enough hours in the day for me to be

able to do my job as a social worker properly *and* date, much less build a relationship with someone who might or might not turn out to be worthwhile," January said in all seriousness.

"Ladies, ladies, this is not the way to behave on the eve of our long postponed and much needed and deserved joint spa weekend," Tatum said as she inevitably picked up the reins of peacemaker.

It was a familiar role for Tatum and one she slipped into time and again. If Simone was the brains and January was the heart and soul of their trio, then Tatum represented their common sense. In addition, it had been Tatum's foresight that had goaded her to open this restaurant in downtown Chicago two years ago. And it had been her determination that helped her turn it into such a success—thanks to her innovative recipes—all in a breathtakingly short amount of time.

All three sisters were dedicated. They all sank long hours and hard work into their chosen fields. It was a work ethic that all three had learned right at home.

"Well, I don't know about you two, but if I don't get some sunshine on this all too pale skin of mine, I'm going to start looking like I've been left out in the rain much too long and I'm starting to rust," January complained.

"Well, don't expect me to feel sorry for you," Simone told her. "Nobody told you to pick up those extra shifts and work all those long hours for the city."

Right, like Simone wouldn't cave the minute she was confronted with a frightened, abused child. "You try looking into those sad little eyes in the faces of the kids I deal with, and you pick which one to say no to. I dare you," January said. She turned toward Tatum. "It's a lot harder, I promise you, than whipping up those sinfully delicious meals for the overprivileged gentry claiming to want to get back to 'nature,'" January told her other sister.

"Ouch," Tatum cried, pretending to wince. "You're tired and overworked, Jan, so I'll cut you some slack. But I'd watch that tongue of yours if I were you."

"I'm sorry. You're right. I am tired and I am overworked." January flashed Tatum an apologetic smile. "I haven't even had time to pack yet."

"You haven't packed yet?" Simone asked, her eyes widening. "Jan, we're leaving in the morning."

"Yes, I am aware of that," January replied wearily. "Just because I don't have a PhD doesn't mean I can't tell time."

"Well, nobody asked me, but I'd say that all three of us are way beyond needing that time off in order to recharge," Tatum told her sisters.

And then she raised her champagne glass, ready to make a toast. When she had reserved this table for their dinner, Tatum had seen to it that the glasses beside the place settings were all filled with their favorite brand of champagne.

"To our much needed vacation," she toasted, her blue eyes affectionately washing over her two best friends—her sisters.

They might have their differences from time to time, but there were no two people she loved more or had greater respect for than her sisters.

Simone followed suit, raising her glass to the others. "To our vacation."

"Our *spa* vacation." January underscored the sentiment, raising her glass, as well.

The sisters clinked their glasses.

"No matter what," Tatum added.

Her sisters echoed the mantra, although both Simone and Tatum did look at January with a hint of suspicion in their eyes.

"Hey, don't look at me like that," January protested. "My boss was the one who insisted I take this vacation, remember?"

"Well, I'll believe it when all three of us are on the plane," Simone said.

"I'll believe it when we're *getting off* the plane," Tatum interjected.

January knew that was for her benefit. "Very funny."

After taking sips of the champagne and then setting down their glasses, the sisters began to eat—and talk excitedly about their plans.

Their voices were intersecting and melding, and at first, they didn't hear the cell phone ringing. When the noise finally penetrated, the sisters looked at one another, silently asking where the ringing was coming from just before they each checked their own device.

And then January held up her hand. "Oh, hold on a second. That is my phone ringing."

Simone exchanged a look with Tatum. "And then there were two," the older sister said with a note of resignation in her voice.

Tatum sighed. This was not the first eleventh-hour

phone call that had ever interrupted their carefully laid plans.

And, most likely, it wouldn't be the last.

Chapter 1

January saw the almost identical leery looks on her sisters' faces as she picked up her cell phone and instinctively knew what they were both thinking.

"It's probably just a last-minute question," she told them.

In general, despite the nature of the sorrow that she dealt with in social services, January was an exceedingly upbeat person. She always saw life in a glass-half-full light. Consequently, January refused to believe that this phone call from her office might possibly be a death knell for her vacation plans. She believed, as she had said, that this was just a last-minute question, either from her boss or her replacement.

Rising from the table, she answered her phone at the same time that she put some space between herself and her sisters. She thought that maybe privacy might be in order. She had learned a long time ago that it was always better to be prepared than to be caught unaware or by surprise.

"Hello, this is January Colton," she told the caller cheerfully. "How may I help you?"

"January, it's Sid Blackwell," the raspy voice on the other end of the call said.

Even if the caller hadn't bothered to identify himself, all he needed to do was say a couple of words and she would have recognized his voice anywhere. It was her boss.

She did her best to dismiss the noticeable sinking sensation in the pit of her stomach that seemed to be mushrooming and said cheerfully, "Hi, Sid, what's up?" and thought it only fair to point out, "I did just leave the office less than forty-five minutes ago."

"I know," she heard her boss say, "and believe me, if there were any other way, I wouldn't be calling you like this, but turns out that this is an unusual situation and frankly, you're the only one I can think of who can help."

He actually sounded contrite, January thought, and that had her worried. After all, Blackwell was the one who had insisted that she take this vacation in the first place.

Something definitely had to be wrong.

January stole a glance over her shoulder. For now, Simone and Tatum weren't paying attention to her. Her sisters seemed busy talking to each other. She breathed a sigh of relief as she turned her head back around.

"All right, Sid, you have my attention," she said, trying to coax Blackwell to get to the point. "Why am I the only one you can think of to handle this?" Maybe her supervisor had just gotten too used to relying on her and this really wasn't as bad as he thought.

"The police just brought in a little girl—she looks like she might be around five-ish," Blackwell said. "Anyway, she was found hiding behind some crates in a warehouse. One of the people in the vicinity called the police when they heard gunfire."

Okay, maybe this *was* as bad as he thought.

"Gunfire?" she asked uneasily. "Is the girl all right?"

"From what I've been told, she appears to be," Blackwell answered. "The detective at the scene thinks the kid might have been a witness to what happened at the warehouse."

"Exactly what happened at the warehouse?" January asked.

"There were three dead bodies—all male—found not too far from where the kid was discovered, cowering," Blackwell told her.

January sucked in her breath. It wasn't hard to envision what that little girl had to have gone through. Alfred Colton's youngest daughter was instantly filled with sympathy.

"That poor thing must be scared out of her mind," January said to her supervisor.

"Must be," Blackwell agreed in his detached sort of way. "The thing is, the detective can't get her to talk. According to what I heard, the kid hasn't said a single word since they found her." January heard her boss pause before finally saying, "I thought that maybe, with all your experience working with special needs children, you might consider just making a quick stop by the police station and monitoring the situation."

Monitoring? Was Blackwell actually saying what she thought he was saying? "Let me get this straight, Sid. Are you *assigning* me to this case?" January asked.

"Oh no, no." She heard her supervisor quickly deny that idea. "Susan Eckhardt is the social worker assigned to this case." Then Blackwell hesitated before he added, "But, well, Susan doesn't have much experience when it comes to special needs children and…"

There was such a thing as too much tiptoeing around a subject, January thought. Blackwell needed to get to the point and call a spade a spade.

"Mr. Blackwell, you and I both know that Susan doesn't have *any* experience when it comes to special needs children."

Rather than argue with her or defend the social worker he had assigned to the case, Blackwell took the easy way out. He focused on the only part that seemed to matter to him.

"Then you'll swing by?" he asked the woman who he acknowledged was one of his best, hardest working employees.

It never occurred to January to turn her boss down, even though, technically she'd already begun her vacation. The child in question had obviously been through something horrible and, at the very least, needed comfort and support. This was what she did very well. She couldn't just get herself to turn away from a child in need.

"Yes, I'll swing by," she told her boss. Taking out her pen and an envelope she had stashed in her purse, January was ready to take notes. "Tell me everything you already know about the case, Sid."

There wasn't all that much.

January listened carefully, jotting down the few facts she felt might be pertinent.

Finished, she told Blackwell, "All right, let Susan know that I'm on my way."

"Thanks, January. I promise I just need a little of your expertise on this matter. You can still start your vacation tomorrow, right?" Blackwell asked her. There was actually a note of hope in his voice.

"Right." *Provided the case doesn't wind up getting more complicated.* Truthfully, January already had her suspicions that it might. "I'll get back to you as soon as I know something," she said just before she terminated the call.

The moment she turned back to face her sisters, she found herself being scrutinized by two sets of very blue eyes. Bracing herself, she sat down for a moment, collecting her thoughts before she said anything.

"Well?" Simone prodded.

January took in a deep breath. "There's been an emergency," she began.

Simone laughed dryly. "That certainly didn't take long." She looked down at her watch.

Tatum just continued looking at January, waiting for the rest of the story to come out. They all knew that there inevitably had to be more.

Her sisters didn't have long to wait.

"The police found a little girl hiding behind some crates in a warehouse," January told them. "It sounds like she might have been a witness to a triple homicide."

Tatum sucked in her breath in horror, immediately envisioning the whole scene in her mind. "Oh, that poor little thing!"

"They can't get her to talk—" January continued as she tried to explain to her sisters why she couldn't turn her supervisor down.

"Well, that's no surprise. The kid's probably really traumatized," Simone told her sisters.

January nodded her head. "That's what I'm thinking," she agreed. "Blackwell said he thinks that she's a special needs child—"

The expression on Tatum's face indicated that she already knew what was coming next.

"And that's your field of expertise, special needs children. Yes, we know," Tatum said. "Go." The restaurateur waved January on her way. "Give us a call later and fill us in on what's going on once you have some kind of a handle on it."

Again, January knew what her sisters were thinking. She could see it in their eyes. They thought that she was getting sucked into something.

"I'm just going in to offer some quick advice to the social worker assigned to the case. This isn't my case," she insisted, looking from one sister to the other.

They didn't believe her. She couldn't blame them. She wasn't buying into it herself, at least not a hundred percent.

"Uh-huh," Tatum murmured.

As January was telling them about the call, Tatum had placed a piece of chicken and several rolls into one of the linen napkins on the table, then wrapped it all up. She pushed the makeshift package toward January.

"Here," she said, offering the linen-wrapped bundle to January. "If this lasts as long as we all know it will, you're going to get hungry."

January sighed, then, rather than demur, she automatically accepted the impromptu care package. "I am *not* staying," she told her sisters emphatically.

"No, of course not," Tatum replied, her expression never changing.

"You keep telling yourself that, kid," Simone said, adding in her two cents. "Don't forget to call at least one of us with an update."

"Right," January agreed. "I'll call you as soon as I leave the police station."

"Uh-huh," her sisters said in unison.

They didn't believe that, either, January thought.

But she meant it. Despite the fact that she had told them that she hadn't packed her suitcase yet, January really was determined to go on this vacation with her sisters.

She had meant what she had said. Other than an occasional lunch on the run, or a quick phone call, it felt as if too much time had elapsed since the three of them had gotten together and just *talked* for any length of time.

Even now, their time together had been interrupted.

All that did for her was reinforce the feeling that they desperately needed some time to catch up. Since the very beginning, they had always been in each other's lives, and just because they were grown women now, that was no excuse for that practice to lapse.

As a matter of fact, there was more reason than ever to reinforce those bonds. January couldn't think of anyone else she wanted to share all the things that she had experienced and was involved in than her sisters. And she wanted to know what was important and going on in their lives, as well.

She thought about her situation and what she might be getting into. No, come hell or high water, by tomorrow morning, she was going to be on board that plane with her sisters so that they could all begin that much anticipated, much needed vacation, January promised herself.

The police station that turned out to be her destination was an old five-story building that had seen more than its share of heartbreak and tragedy. Just the sight of it as she turned the corner and approached it in her car fostered a sadness within her.

January tried to see the building through the eyes of a child, and she found it hard not to shiver—or cry for that matter.

That poor little girl, January couldn't help thinking. More than likely, the child hoped this was all just a bad dream.

She caught herself wondering if the little girl was related to any of the dead men who had been found at the warehouse. That could very well explain why the child had shut herself off and wasn't saying anything. That kind of shock had been known to cause amnesia in an adult. How much more powerful could that reaction turn out to be if it was a child witnessing that sort of crime instead?

January really hoped that she would be able to help this child. Never mind getting her to remember and volunteer any sort of information about what happened to those men at the warehouse—*if* it turned out that the little girl had actually witnessed anything. January was far more concerned about being able to reach the child before she submerged herself in some sort of fantasy world that was totally outside the realm of reality.

Gearing herself up mentally, January hurried up the stairs, her high heels clicking against the cement. She normally dressed a little more conservatively when she worked, but since she'd been meeting her sisters after work and this really was a special occasion, for once January had dressed a little fancier than she usually did.

Pushing the glass and metal-framed door open, she stepped inside the police station. She was immediately met by a wall of ever-present noise as well as an uncomfortable warmth, despite the fact that this was winter in Chicago.

January was aware of several pairs of eyes looking in her direction. A couple displayed moderate interest before turning away and getting back to whatever had their attention at the moment.

Not wanting to waste any unnecessary time, she quickly approached the front desk and the sergeant behind it.

Hopefully, Blackwell had called ahead the way she had asked him to do. Smiling at the tall, bald, uniformed man at the desk, January took out her wallet. She flipped to her identification and held it up for the sergeant to see.

"Hi. I'm not sure if my supervisor called ahead to let you know I was coming, but I'm January Colton with Child Protective Services. I was told that one of your detectives brought in a little girl earlier. She was found at the scene of a triple homicide," she added, thinking that would jar the sergeant's memory.

The desk sergeant nodded his head. "Oh, you must mean Detective Stafford."

"I'm sorry, I'm afraid I don't know his name. I was just told that he was the one who found and brought in a little girl—"

"Yes, he did," the sergeant recalled. His brown eyes met hers. "The one who hasn't spoken. Detective Stafford called in a social worker to get the kid to talk, but so far, nobody's had any luck." Lowering his voice, he confided, "The social worker is stymied. She hasn't been able to get the kid to say a word."

January nodded her head. "I know. My supervisor told me. That's why he asked me to come by and see if I had any better luck at getting the girl to talk. Do you think you might be able to call this Detective Stafford out here so I could talk to him? Or better yet, tell me where I can find the little girl and I'll take it from there."

But the desk sergeant shook his head. "I'm afraid I can't do that, ma'am. There are regulations to follow."

This was not what she needed at the end of the day. Blackwell was supposed to have resolved this. "I realize that, Sergeant. But I *have* been here before," January stressed.

The sergeant squinted his eyes as he looked at her. "I'm sorry, I don't recognize you—"

"And I don't recognize you." She took out her identification again and held it up closer for his review. "But I'm willing to talk to you. Look—Sergeant Wilkerson," she said, reading the tag on his shirt, "there's a very frightened little girl somewhere in your station and I'd like to connect with her so that I can help her be less frightened. Do you think you can help me do that?"

The sergeant sighed just as someone else approached him with a question. The policeman started talking, but Wilkerson held up his hand, signaling for the police officer to back off.

"Wait your turn, Andrews," he snapped. "Can't you see that there's someone ahead of you?"

She could see this quickly escalating into a heated argument. "Look, I don't want to cause any problems or interfere, Sergeant Wilkerson. You obviously have your hands full here. If you could just point me in the right direction, I promise I'll get out of your hair."

"Good one," the policeman laughed, glancing toward his partner.

The desk sergeant might have been bald, but his eyebrows were very full and bushy. They drew together now as he scowled at the police officer. "What did you say?" Wilkerson challenged him.

She was used to refereeing squabbling children and this really wasn't all that different. January raised her voice. "We're getting off topic here, gentlemen," she told the two police officers. When both men looked at her in surprise, January decided to approach the problem from a different angle.

Locking eyes with the desk sergeant, she said, "Look, if you could either call this Detective Stafford to come down to the front desk, or point me in the direction where I can find him, I can get down to what's really important here—getting that little girl to tell someone what she saw."

Wilkerson laughed. The sound had no humor in it. "Good luck with that," he told her. "I saw him trying to get her to talk to him about *anything* when he brought her in. It's like she was in her own little world." He leaned over the desk, although his voice didn't get any lower. "You ask me, it's like she's really spooked."

"She probably just saw three men get shot and killed, maybe even right in front of her. If that happened to you when you were a little kid, my guess is that you'd be spooked, too," a tall, dark-haired and ruggedly handsome man said as he approached the front desk from the far right.

Ah, January thought as she turned toward the man who had just walked in to get a closer look. *Detective Stafford, I presume.*

Chapter 2

"And you'd be right," January told the man who was now standing almost next to her.

The detective had a larger-than-life presence, even though in her estimation he was probably only about three inches taller than she was, and she was wearing three-inch heels.

January put out her hand to the detective.

"Sid Blackwell sent me," she told Stafford by way of an introduction. "My name is January Colton and as you've probably already guessed, I'm with the Department of Social Services."

Sean blinked as he suddenly got a good look at her and became aware of the vivacious, classy blonde standing in front of the desk sergeant. In his estimation, she looked more like a model than a social worker—

and young, quite young. She certainly didn't look old enough to be a social worker.

His eyes met and held hers. After a beat, the detective took the hand that she was offering.

January caught herself thinking that the sexy detective's grip felt strong, but not overpowering. There was something about him that seemed genuine. She decided that she liked him.

"Nice to meet you, Ms. Colton," Sean said. His smile was tight, but polite. "I'm assuming that Blackwell told you what the problem seems to be."

"He did, but sometimes things get lost or omitted if a third party is involved," January told the detective. "Why don't you tell me about the problem in your own words?"

What January was trying to get was the detective's perspective on the situation. She had learned that a lot of things could be revealed through the words a person used or didn't use. Besides, the detective had been at the scene and her supervisor hadn't been.

Sean was about to tell the woman that, since she already seemed to know what was going on, he wasn't about to jump through hoops just for her personal amusement. But he also knew that was just his frustration talking. So, instead, the homicide detective took the social worker aside so he could talk to her and fill her in on the details away from the desk sergeant and anyone else who might be listening.

"We got a call from someone in the area claiming that they heard shots being fired at the old, abandoned toy warehouse. The patrolmen who took the call figured it was probably just a car backfiring, but because the call was logged in, they had to go to the location and check it out." The detective's expression was grim as he told her, "When they did, they weren't prepared for what they found. Three adult males, shot dead."

January tried not to wince. Because of her job, she was used to dealing with abuse in various forms, but so far, she had never had to deal with murder. This was something new for her.

"They were murdered, I take it?" she asked. That was what she had been told, but somehow, saying it out loud made it that much more real for her. January's breath felt as if it had just solidified and backed up in her throat.

Sean caught himself studying this woman.

Closely.

Judging from her clothes and her bearing, she looked a little too polished to be doing this sort of work for a living. Given her last name, Sean couldn't help wondering if this was all just a diverting lark for her, or if she actually took this job seriously.

Belatedly, he realized that the social worker had asked him a question and that he hadn't answered her.

Nodding, he said, "Yes, they were murdered. Execution style," he added, watching her face for a reaction.

To her credit, the woman seemed to take the news in stride. "How was the little girl found?" she asked.

"The coroner was just logging the bodies in," Sean answered, "when his assistant heard this high-pitched whimpering noise coming from not too far off."

"Whimpering?" January asked. She could almost

picture the scenario and her heart ached for the fright-ened little girl.

Sean nodded. "One of the patrol officers said it sounded a little like a frightened puppy. Thinking it might be another victim too weak to call out, the re-sponding officers spread out, looking for him or her." The detective frowned as he described the scene. "They found Annie crouching behind some crates, apparently attempting to hide."

"Annie," January repeated. Blackwell had told her that no one knew who the little girl was. Had he made a mistake? "Then you found out her name?" she asked, curious.

The detective shook his head. "No. One of the patrol-men referred to her as Annie. You know, like Orphan Annie, the kid in that old comic strip," Sean explained.

"I know who Orphan Annie is," she told the detec-tive. "So did she respond to that name when you called her Annie?"

The detective shook his head. "No, and that's part of the reason why you're here. As far as I know, Annie, or whatever her real name is, hasn't responded to *anything* that has been said to her. I tried to get her to talk, but it was like I wasn't even there. The social worker your department sent tried her hand at communicating with the kid, but she didn't get anywhere, either.

"As a matter of fact, after she made several attempts to get the little girl to say something, *anything*, your Ms. Eckhardt got this confounded look on her face like she felt she was completely out of her depth. I got the im-pression that she was afraid to call her supervisor about it, so I did. Seemed like the best way to go. Blackwell said he would send reinforcements. Apparently—" Sean gestured at her "—you're the reinforcements."

Okay, January thought. She needed to clear a few things up for this detective.

"First of all, she's not *my* Ms. Eckhardt. We just work in the same department and I've been there a couple of years longer than Susan has," she began to explain.

Sean held up his hand, stopping the social worker before she could continue. "No offense, but I don't need—or want—your whole backstory here," he told January impatiently. "What I *do* need to know is the kid's backstory and the sooner you can help me get that, the sooner I can start piecing together what happened in that warehouse today, as well as finding out who shot those men and *why* they were shot."

January waited until the detective paused to take a breath and then she surprised him by laughing at his agenda. "You're not asking for much now, are you?"

Sean's eyes met hers. It was almost a contest of wills. Neither one looked away. "Not if you're as good as I was told you were," the detective responded.

January eyed him a little uncertainly. Was he just trying to use flattery on her, or was he actually telling her the truth? "And just who told you this? That I was good," she clarified. She didn't think that Susan would have said something like that. The social worker was too involved in moving up to waste any compliments on her coworkers.

"Your boss. Blackwell."

That surprised her. Blackwell wasn't generous when it came to handing out compliments.

As if reading her mind, the detective said, "And if you don't believe me, that nervous social worker I left with my half-pint witness confirmed it when I asked her about you—before I was 'summoned' to come get you."

January focused on one term: *witness*. "I thought you said that you weren't sure if the little girl witnessed the shootings or not," January said, recalling what Blackwell had passed on to her from his conversation with the detective.

For the first time, she saw the detective grin. It was like watching beams of warm sunlight stretching out and brightening the immediate world.

"Hey, what can I say? I'm an optimist," the detective said with a shrug.

"Thinking that a little girl is the key witness to multiple homicides and then viewing that as being optimistic wouldn't be the way I'd describe it," January informed him.

The detective noted the cool tone of her voice.

"I'm not heartless," he told January. He wasn't sure why it seemed so important to him that she know that, but it was. "The way I see it, this gives me a way to get the jump on whoever did this and allows me to eliminate the threat against the kid at the same time."

"Threat?" January repeated uncertainly.

"Threat," Sean said again. "Because, trust me, if the killer even *suspects* that he was caught in the act and that there is the smallest possibility that 'Annie' here can identify him, her life won't be worth the proverbial plugged nickel."

January found that promise completely unnerving. "Well, since you put it so bluntly, let's go talk to her, shall we?" she urged the detective. "In my experience, kids are like sponges. They absorb everything and anything around them and—barring a really traumatic incident—they are usually able to recreate what they saw, at least to a reasonable degree."

"We have her in one of the interview rooms," he told her. "Your Ms. Eck—" Sean stopped himself and began again, this time correcting his initial mistake. "Ms. Eckhardt is in there with the little girl."

January hardly heard him. She had been at this station a couple of times before, but each time she had only gotten as far as the front desk or somewhere in that general vicinity. She had never been asked to go into the police station proper before. Certainly not to one of the interview rooms.

As she followed the detective now, she scanned the surrounding area. January found it to be exceedingly depressing, what with its drab, faded pea soup green walls and its decidedly oppressive atmosphere. She caught herself thinking that a weak-willed person would confess to almost anything if it meant that they could get out of here.

"When was the last time this place was painted?" she asked the detective.

The question seemed to come out of the blue, catching Sean off guard. He looked at her to see if he'd heard wrong for some reason.

"Why would you ask something like that?" he asked.

"Because just look at this place," she told him, gesturing around at the walls as they continued to make their way down the hall. "It's depressing."

"Our chief objective at the station isn't to make people happy," Sean told her, still thinking her question rather odd.

"You know," she said speculatively, "you might want to think that strategy over. If the people you're questioning are in a better frame of mind, it might make them more willing to respond to what you're asking in a positive light. It might make them want to cooperate. Just a thought," she added quickly before the detective could become defensive—or worse. She didn't want to make him combative; she was trying to offer some constructive criticism.

"I'll pass your suggestion along to the police station's interior decorator," Sean said.

"You do that," she responded. "So where's the interview room?" It seemed to her that they had been walking for a while now and she didn't see anything that came close to looking like an interview room.

"It's on the next floor," he told her just as they came to an elevator. Stopping, Sean pressed the button.

January heard the elevator approaching. It was making a grinding noise that was far from soothing.

"If it's just on the next floor, we could take the stairs," she suggested.

Just as she said that, the elevator came to a halt. The door opened, albeit almost in what appeared to be slow motion.

This was a really bad omen, January couldn't help thinking.

"You don't mind?" Sean asked, responding to her suggestion to take the stairs.

The elevator looked almost ancient, January thought, glancing into it. "I'm just thinking in terms of expediency."

Sean shrugged. "Well, it's here now," he pointed out. "We might as well take it."

If it had been up to her, she would have taken the stairs. But January didn't feel like arguing about it. She was sure that there would be other things to argue about with this detective soon enough.

"Whatever you say," she said philosophically as she walked into the elevator ahead of him.

Was it her imagination, or did she hear the elevator creak?

"Oh, if only," Sean murmured under his breath in response to her comment as she walked into the elevator.

Having entered the small elevator car, January turned to look at him. "Excuse me?"

"Nothing," the detective answered. "Just commenting in general." With that, Sean reached around January and pressed the button for the second floor.

"It's been a long day," he explained, since she was obviously waiting for more.

January gave him the benefit of the doubt. He was probably referring to the triple homicide he had caught—and his uncommunicative possible witness.

"So I gather." She thought about why she was there.

"I'll see what I can do to get your witness to open up and talk."

The detective nodded. He believed her. "I'd appreciate it," he told her with sincerity.

The elevator door seemed to close in slow motion, just the way it had opened. Then it appeared as if it was thinking about its next move. He reached around her again and pressed the button a second time.

When still nothing happened, January asked, "Is the elevator thinking it over?"

"Sometimes it's slow to respond," Sean told her, frowning slightly.

"Maybe it wants you to pick a different floor," she cracked. When the elevator continued to remain where it was, door closed but not moving, January had another suggestion. "Maybe we should just have the elevator open its doors again. If we had taken the stairs, we'd already be there."

As far as she was concerned, they were pushing their luck.

Just then, the elevator suddenly came to life. It lurched, and then moved upward, inching its way along. "It just takes patience," Sean told her, although it was clear that he was running out of his.

"What it could probably take is getting a complete overhaul," she responded. "Maybe if it had that, then it would run more smoothly."

"Yeah, that, too," Sean agreed.

The words were no sooner out of his mouth than the elevator came to an abrupt, jarring stop.

January waited expectantly in front of the door,

but it didn't open, even though the whining, grinding noise that the elevator had been making had completely ceased.

The door still didn't budge. "Are we there yet or not?" she asked Sean.

He bit back a terse response and just said, "No way of knowing."

They both looked up at the top of the elevator. The light that indicated which floor they had reached had gone out, giving no indication as to whether or not they had come to their destination or if the journey had been suddenly aborted between floors without any warning.

"My guess is 'not,'" she said, still looking up at the unlit array of numbers at the top of the elevator. The numbers that were supposed to alert them as to what floor they were coming to.

"Certainly looks that way," the detective agreed.

"Okay, now what?" January asked, turning toward the man.

Sean sighed as he opened the small, metal door that housed the phone to call for help.

"Now we call maintenance to let them know that we're stuck here and to send someone to get this tin box moving again." Sean didn't bother looking at her, but he could feel the woman's green eyes on him. "And yes, I know. You were right," he conceded, albeit unwillingly. "We should have taken the stairs."

She didn't think he would acknowledge that so quickly and she felt a certain amount of satisfaction because he did. It allowed her to be magnanimous.

"I didn't say a word," January told him innocently.

"But you were thinking it," he said with certainty, growing more impatient as he waited for someone on the other end of the line to pick up. He didn't feel like standing here like this. He wanted someone to come to their aid and get this damn elevator running. The stalled car was growing stuffy.

January didn't particularly care for the detective's attitude. "If you're that good at reading minds, why did you need me to come here and deal with your witness?"

The last thing he needed was a wisecracking social worker. "Look, lady—"

"Back it up, Detective," she said sharply. "My name is January, not *lady*," she informed him. There was something very impersonal and almost insulting to her about being addressed as "lady." She felt as if he was saying she didn't care or get down in the trenches in order to work hard on her cases so she could solve whatever problem had reared its defiant, spiky little head.

Sean backed away and nodded. "January," he said obligingly. "I called Child Services because Eckhardt wasn't up to doing her job and I thought that maybe if I made the call, it would carry more weight."

"Mystery solved," she declared glibly, smiling a little too brightly at him.

"One of them, anyway," he murmured. Sean frowned at the phone. It was still ringing. No one was picking it up on the other end. "Where is everyone?" he asked irritably as it rang again.

"Probably having dinner would be my guess." She looked up at the elevator ceiling and tossed him an idea.

"Listen, if I stand on your shoulders, I could probably get that trapdoor open."

January didn't actually see the detective staring at her in speechless wonder—but she could swear that she felt him doing it.

Chapter 3

"And then what?" Sean finally asked. He couldn't begin to imagine this long-haired, blond vision in the light blue dress and high heels actually climbing up on his shoulders, much less pushing open the trapdoor right above their heads.

January barely glanced in the detective's direction. She couldn't help thinking that, for a detective, he didn't have much of an imagination. "And then I see just how far between floors the elevator actually is."

Sean continued to watch her, utterly fascinated. Just how far was this woman prepared to go with this superheroine fantasy of hers? "And then what?" he asked her again, this time supplying a guess. "You shimmy up the cables to get to that landing?"

January sighed. Obviously, this man was *not* prepared to do anything about their situation.

"Unless you have a better idea," she told him. Maybe he didn't grasp the full import of this. "Look, there's a frightened little girl one floor above us. Getting to her and comforting her is my only objective at the moment."

He came across a lot of people in his line of work. This woman sounded as if she was nothing short of a crusader. Great, just what he needed. "You really mean that."

"Of course I mean it. I'm not playing games here, Detective. Now boost me up so I can climb onto your shoulders," she told him as she looked up at the ceiling.

But instead of doing as she asked, Stafford just smiled at her.

"Why are you grinning like that?" January asked, growing more impatient by the minute.

"As intriguing and appealing as the idea of having you sitting astride my shoulders is, I think it might be simpler if I just talked to maintenance."

As she began to point out what was wrong with that idea—he had just told her that no one was picking up—Sean cut her short by pointing to the receiver and saying, "Someone finally answered the phone."

And then he turned his attention to the person on the other end of the line. "Yes, hi," Sean said. "This is Detective Stafford. Social Worker Colton and I are stuck in elevator number three. It stopped moving between the first and second floors. Uh-huh. Okay, do what you have to do to get this thing moving before we grow old in here. Thanks."

January blew out a breath. "So?" she asked. "How long did whoever answered you say it was going to take them to get this thing moving again?" As good-looking as the man was, she didn't welcome the idea of being stuck with him in this elevator for an indefinite period of time. "Because if he thinks they can't fix the problem for a number of hours, I'm still willing to give it a try my way," she told him.

The woman was obviously stubbornness personified, Sean thought. He wasn't sure if that was a good thing or not. He was about to repeat what the maintenance man he had spoken to had told him when the elevator suddenly lurched again. Without any warning, Sean found himself colliding with her. He grabbed January by the shoulders to prevent any sort of real damage or injury.

"Sorry," he apologized, releasing her as the elevator car began to move arthritically to the next floor. "Are you all right?" he asked, his eyes taking inventory very carefully as he looked January over.

"Yes, I'm fine," she answered almost haltingly, obviously trying to get her bearings.

"I'll take a rain check on those proposed acrobatics just in case this doesn't pan out," Sean told her, referring to the revived elevator car.

She frowned. "Very funny."

"No, I'm serious," he told her. "I think I'd like to see you in action."

"The elevator appears to have come back to life. But I'm taking the stairs down after I interview that girl," she informed the detective.

"Understood." They reached the next floor and the

elevator door slowly opened. Sean put his hand out against it, ensuring that the door remained opened and secured in place.

January stepped out quickly. He followed right behind her. "Let me guess," he said as he led the way to the interview rooms. "You were the youngest in a family of all boys."

"You got the youngest part right," January told him. "But I had two sisters. No brothers."

His brow furrowed a little as he tried to make sense of what she was saying. Why would she be so competitive if there were no brothers egging her on? "Then I don't understand," he confessed.

"You don't need to understand, Detective Stafford. All you need to know is that I'm very agile if the situation calls for it."

She'd made the comment in complete innocence. But the way the detective smiled at her told her that he hadn't taken it in that light.

She shouldn't have said anything, she thought.

"Good to know," Sean told her. And then his smile faded as he approached the interview room where he had left the other social worker and the little girl she had been sent to help.

He found himself hoping that this woman turned out to be more helpful than the first one.

Relief washed over Susan Eckhardt's rounded face as she caught sight of the detective through the upper, glass portion of the door. By the time Sean quietly opened the door, the social worker was on her feet and at the threshold.

"I was beginning to think that maybe you weren't coming back," she told him.

If she hadn't known better, January would have said that the other social worker was flirting with the detective.

"Hello, Susan," January said, nodding at the other woman.

Any thoughts of a continued flirtation seemed to instantly vanish as Susan drew back her shoulders. "January, I heard you were supposed to be on vacation."

"Rumors of my vacation are greatly exaggerated," January quipped, and then smiled a little wearily. "It actually starts tomorrow. Sid called and said you caught a difficult case."

Susan rolled her eyes as she glanced back at the little girl who wasn't facing them. She seemed preoccupied with something on the back wall. "You can say that again. I can't get the kid to talk to me or even acknowledge me."

January thought of what she would have done. "You've tried to talk to her about something simple?" she asked the other social worker.

Susan grew slightly irritated. "I'm not a newbie. Of course I did."

"And?" January pressed. She wanted any input that Susan could provide.

Susan raised and lowered her wide shoulders in a helpless manner. "And nothing. It's like I'm not even there." She blew out an exasperated breath. "If I wanted to be ignored, I would have stayed married to Geoff," she said, frustrated. And then she looked at the detective. She obviously didn't want him thinking that she was involved with anyone. "Geoff's my ex-husband."

"I kind of gathered that." Sean noticed that the woman who had been so ready to do acrobatics to get them out of the stalled elevator wasn't saying anything. She seemed to be observing the little girl he had brought back with him. The little girl was wandering around the other end of the room, completely oblivious to them.

"When I found her, she was all but curled up in a ball," he told January. "Like she was trying to pull into herself. It was almost as if she was trying to become invisible."

January nodded her head. "That's kind of theme and variation on the concept some kids have that if they close their eyes and don't see you, you can't see them." She continued to thoughtfully regard the nameless little girl.

Then she turned toward the two other adults in the room. "And she's made no attempt to say anything to either of you?"

"Not a word," Susan answered. And then the woman laughed to herself. "You'd think that would be rather refreshing after some of the kids we have to deal with, you know? But the silent treatment gets old really fast, too."

January was only half listening to Susan. Her eyes on the little girl, January approached her slowly. The child still had her back to her when January started talking in a low, nonthreatening tone.

"Hi, my name's January. Like the month," she said, since so many children had commented on her name, saying it was funny or odd. "It's kind of silly, I know, but my mom was hoping for a boy and she didn't have any names ready for a girl. She just looked at the calendar and picked that one."

The entire time she was talking to the child, the little girl was making no response. She didn't even turn around to acknowledge the fact that she was being spoken to.

January thought that was a little odd—and possibly telling.

"See?" Susan said, irritated as she gestured toward the girl's back. "She's rude."

"Or scared," Sean countered.

But January was beginning to suspect that there was a third alternative to this scenario. Turning toward them, she said as much. "Or deaf."

Susan's head jerked up. It was clear by the expression on her face that that possibility had never occurred to her.

"You think she's deaf?" Sean asked, surprised. That thought hadn't occurred to him, either.

"Very possibly," January answered, cautiously approaching the little girl who still had her back to them. "If she's deaf, that would explain why she didn't look toward the door when we walked in. She was looking away at the time—and didn't hear it."

Coming up behind the girl now, January lightly tapped her on the shoulder. The little girl almost jumped out of her skin as she whirled around to look at who had come up behind her, her braided brown hair flying.

There was a look of utter surprise on her face. It was apparent that she hadn't realized that there were two more people in the room now than there had been a moment ago. It was also obvious to January that the little girl had not connected with Susan in any fashion, but she looked very happy to see Sean.

The little girl quickly crossed the floor to get to him and then shyly wrapped her arms around his waist, or what she could reach of it.

"If you ask me, I'd say that you made a real connection with your potential witness," January told him.

Sean appeared to be surprised by the social worker's conclusion. "I thought she was just responding to the fact that I carried her in here."

"There's that, yes, but in her limited little world, you also represent her only friend right now," January pointed out.

Watching Sean, she saw him smiling at the little girl. It wasn't a patronizing smile, or one that was being forced out of some sense of obligation. January liked to think that she could tell the difference and she noticed that his eyes were smiling at the child.

"Not only that," January added. "But she senses that you're a good man."

Susan turned her thousand-watt smile on Sean, as well. "Yeah, me too," she said, adding her voice to the tally.

January frowned. She didn't have time for whatever this was devolving into. Nor did she have the patience for it, not when there was a genuine, real problem before them. She made a snap decision.

"Susan, I've got this," January said, glancing at her

watch. "It's getting late. Why don't you go home? It's way past the end of your day."

The suggestion was met with instant relief. "You don't mind?" the other woman asked, barely able to contain her eagerness.

"No, of course not. I wouldn't have said it if I did." January waved the other woman toward the door. "Go home." And as the other women began to leave, she called after her. "And Susan?"

The younger woman stopped in her tracks and turned around. "Yes?"

"You might want to think about a change in careers," January suggested.

Susan frowned, briefly torn and confused. But that quickly faded. Coming to, she lost no time in leaving the room.

As Susan closed the door behind her, January saw Sean looking at her quizzically. She could almost read the question in his eyes.

"I told her to go home because she wasn't being any help and I got the sense that she was growing more and more frustrated with the whole situation. Not to mention the fact that she didn't seem to realize that this little doll was deaf. That was rather sad," she told him.

"I didn't realize it, either," the detective pointed out.

"Yes, but you thought she was traumatized, and you did have a lot of other things going on at the same time, like a triple murder. It's not your job to be in tune with a scared little girl who can't hear you speaking to her. It is, however, part of Susan's job, as it is part of all our jobs in social services."

The sight of the little girl curled up on his lap warmed her heart. It told her that despite the detective's tough-guy act, there was a warm human being beneath that exterior facade.

"So now what do we do?" Sean asked, looking at January above the little girl's head. "How do we go about communicating with her?"

She gazed down compassionately. "Well, hopefully, someone taught her how to sign."

"You mean talking with her hands?" Sean asked, admittedly out of his depth here.

January smiled at the detective, nodding in response to his question. "Exactly."

The little girl looked as if she was falling asleep on his lap. He had never given having children a second thought—until just now. "Isn't she a little young to know how to do that?"

"The younger they are, the easier a time they have learning something. The school of thought is that foreign languages should be taught to children when they're very young. Signing is just another form of a foreign language," she told him. "Hopefully, her parents or parent was smart enough to get her into some sort of program as soon as they realized that she was unable to hear anything or anyone."

"Maybe she's not deaf," he said, thinking the matter over. "Maybe she's just blocking everything out because she was so traumatized and she doesn't want to deal with anything."

Rather than answer the detective, January took several steps back. "Annie" had her face buried against

Sean's chest. It was turned away from her. Taking in a deep breath, January let loose with an ear-splitting whistle.

There was no reaction on the little girl's part.

January looked up at the detective. "She's deaf, all right," she told him.

Sean, in turn, looked down at the child he was holding. There was a sadness in his eyes. "I guess she is," he agreed, then forced himself to move on. "I take it that you know how to sign?"

January smiled at him. "Yes, I do. Luckily, I made learning that as part of my training. There are more hearing-impaired, or partially hearing-impaired children, in the social services system than you might think. Working within this system also brings one to the inevitable conclusion that there are parents out there who should have never become parents."

She shivered as she thought the matter over. "Sometimes they take out their frustrations on their children in ways that are absolutely horrifying. Thank heaven that I have a family that not only keeps me grounded, but also makes me mindful that there is a brighter, more optimistic side to life. I sometimes cling to that, especially when I'm dealing with children who have been abandoned."

He raised his eyes to January's. "So you *do* know how to communicate with her?"

She smiled at the detective. "If she knows signing, I do."

"And if she doesn't?" Sean pressed.

She was up for that, too, if she had to be. "Then I'll find an alternate way to communicate with her."

"But wait a minute." Sean suddenly remembered something. "Didn't that other social worker say you were going on vacation tomorrow?"

"No," January corrected him, "she thought I was already *on* vacation. It technically wasn't supposed to start until tomorrow."

"Okay, so it starts tomorrow," he said, going along with her explanation. "If that's the case, how can you help? You're not going to be around to work with her." Sean nodded at the sleeping girl.

January had already considered that. Being exposed to the child had convinced her that she couldn't just abandon her.

"Regarding my vacation, there's no requirement as to where I can take it," she informed him. "Which means I can choose to take it in my house if that's how things play themselves out."

He stared at her, surprised. "So is that what you're planning to do?"

January looked down at the sleeping child, a smile playing on her lips. "I think so."

Chapter 4

The little girl stirred on the detective's lap. One moment she appeared to be sleeping peacefully, the next, her eyes flew open. She looked surprised, as if she didn't know where she was and was desperately trying to figure it out.

As she scrambled up into a sitting position, her large light-brown eyes darted back and forth, moving from Sean to January and then back again. Her agitation escalated by the second.

"Can you communicate with her, let her know she's safe?" Sean asked, doing his best to try to calm the little girl down by rocking back and forth in a soothing, comforting motion.

"I can certainly try," January answered.

Okay, here goes nothing, she thought as she tapped

the little girl on the shoulder to get her attention. Huge fearful eyes looked up at January.

January smiled at her, then brought her fingers and thumb together and tapped them to her lips several times. Then extended the sign to include Sean.

To her relief, the little girl seemed to understand. She bobbed her head up and down as a small smile blossomed on her lips.

"What just happened here?" Sean asked. He didn't like being kept in the dark and this was a world he knew nothing about.

January's triumphant smile was nothing short of dazzling as she turned toward the detective. "I think we've just had a breakthrough, Detective." She smiled warmly at the little girl. "She does know how to sign."

"Are you sure?" he asked. "Did you just communicate with her?" When it had become clear that the little girl was deaf, he had thought that getting through to her would be really difficult. She represented a whole new, mysterious world to him. Now, judging by the smile on the small face, there was hope.

"Yes I did. I asked her if she wanted to eat and she said yes," January informed him happily. "Well, she nodded yes. But it's practically the same thing."

"But she can understand you?" Sean asked, wanting to be perfectly clear on this. His eyes never left January's face. If she was lying for some reason, maybe to bolster her own self-image, he would know.

The social worker's green eyes crinkled. "It would appear that she does," she answered. She was so genuinely happy about the matter, she was positively glowing.

As far as Sean was concerned, they had just dipped their toes in the water. Now the real work began. He had a whole list of things he wanted to know. "Can you find out her name?" he asked eagerly.

She wanted to tell him to take things slowly, but she sensed that he wouldn't take well to that. He would probably think she was trying to tell him his job. So, instead, she decided to make a suggestion.

"Why don't we get her something to eat and then, once she has something in her stomach, we can try to get some information from her—like her name." January watched the detective's face to see if what she was proposing irritated him.

Sean could barely harness his impatience, but he also knew that she was right. "Okay," he agreed. "I'll get her something to eat." He began to leave but he heard January call out after him.

"Detective?"

Sean stopped just short of the doorway and turned around. "Yes?"

"Don't take the elevator. If the vending machines are on another floor, you need to be able to come back. So make sure you use the stairs," January suggested.

The detective nodded his head. "Point taken," he acknowledged.

But as he started to leave the interrogation room for a second time, the little girl at the center of this drama broke away from January. Dashing up to him, the child wrapped her arms around his leg.

"Looks like someone doesn't want you to go," January commented, her mouth curving in an amused smile.

"I tell you what. Tell me where the vending machines are located and I'll go get her something to eat."

Sean slowly returned to the table, careful not to cause the little girl to tumble backward. "That wouldn't be very gallant of me, sending you," he told January before taking out his cell phone.

She thought that was rather an odd thing for him to say. She had to admit that the detective and the little girl made quite a picture together.

"I didn't realize being gallant was in play here," January told him.

"Being gallant is *always* in play," he remarked. Reaching the party he was calling, his focus shifted. "Hey, Martinez." Detective Eric Martinez was the man he occasionally partnered with since his old partner had left the Homicide Division. "I didn't think you'd still be here."

"Actually, I'm not," Eric answered. "I'm just on my way out."

"Well, this won't take long. I need you to get a sandwich and a soda from the vending machine and bring it to the second-floor interview room. No, it's not for me," Sean assured him when Eric made a comment about being his errand boy. "It's for a potential witness to those warehouse murders I caught today. And don't forget the soda," he told Martinez, thinking the little girl had to be thirsty.

She smiled at him, as if she somehow knew what he was doing. "Oh, and see if you can find some cookies, too. Any kind of cookies," Sean said in response to the question the other detective asked.

Terminating the call, Sean put his phone back in his pocket. "Okay, that's taken care of. Food's on its way." He looked down at the little girl and repeated what he had just said, moving his lips very slowly. Then he felt foolish. "She probably doesn't read lips, does she?" he asked January.

"She might," the social worker answered. "But right now, we have no way of knowing one way or another. Like I said, after she eats, maybe we can find answers to some of the rest of the questions that come up."

Just then, the little girl pulled the bottom of Sean's jacket. When he looked at her, the little girl hooked both of her pointer fingers together in an X, then switched their positions.

Sean looked at her hands in confusion, then raised his eyes to January's face. "Is she trying to tell me something?"

"I think so," she answered the detective. January couldn't help grinning broadly. "She just called you her friend."

"Is that what that means?" he asked, nodding at the little girl's hands.

January inclined her head. The child had obviously connected with the detective. This would make things easier in the long run, she hoped. "Yes."

And then, to her surprise, she watched as Sean did his best to mimic what the girl had signed to him.

"Did I get it right?" he asked January, still looking at the little girl.

January smiled at her and then at Sean. "I think that big grin on her face should answer your question."

She saw a similar expression totally encompass his face. "You're right," he replied.

Just then, there was a knock on the door. Opening it without waiting to be invited in, Detective Eric Martinez walked in, a wrapped sandwich and bag of cookies in one hand, a can of soda in the other.

"I brought you that sandwich, cookies and soda you asked for," Eric announced. "Is this your hot date, Stafford?" he asked, smiling broadly at the little girl. "Hi, honey," he said to her.

"Save your breath, Martinez. Your charm is wasted here," Sean told his partner, taking the items from him. "She can't hear you."

"Haven't you heard?" the other detective asked, making eye contact with the little girl. He smiled broadly at her and she shyly returned the smile. "Charm transcends words."

"Uh-huh. What do I owe you?" Sean asked as he placed the sandwich, cookies and soda on the table in front of the little girl.

"That's okay," Eric answered. "I think I can cover this magnificent spread."

Meanwhile, the little girl was looking at the food hungrily, but she made no attempt to pick up anything. January tapped her on the shoulder and signed for the little girl to eat.

Beaming, the little girl picked up the cookies. But before she could tear open the plastic bag, January shook her head and indicated that she needed to eat the sandwich first.

The child's eyes darted toward Sean, who nodded

his agreement. The little girl bobbed her head up and down, and then picked up the food. The bright brown eyes looked from January to the detective, as if to make sure they were both in agreement. When they both nodded at her, the little girl happily sank her teeth into the sandwich.

"Looks like you both speak her language," Martinez observed.

"This part doesn't take much," January replied. "The rest of it might be harder, though."

"And you are…?" Eric asked, raising one brow as he waited to be filled in.

Sean did the honors. "This is January Colton. She's the social worker that children's services sent to work with this little girl."

"She the one you found hiding in the warehouse?" Eric asked.

Sean nodded. "One and the same."

Martinez had more questions, and he knew who to direct them to. He turned toward the social worker. "You think you can get her to tell you what we need to know?" he asked her.

"All I can do is try—provided she does know something." January watched as the little girl consumed her food. For a hungry child, she ate rather daintily, January couldn't help thinking. Someone had definitely taught her manners. "You forget, she might not have seen anything going down. You said she was found hiding behind the crates, which were some distance away from where the bodies were discovered," she recalled.

Eric nodded. "That's what I heard." He turned toward Sean. "Well, keep me posted if you do find out anything," he said. Eric paused to smile at the little girl as he told Sean, "I've got to get going. It's Alicia's third birthday and Rachel will absolutely skin me alive if I don't show up until after she's tucked in bed and sound asleep."

Sean nodded, gesturing for his partner to be on his way. "Go," he urged. "Give my best to Rachel."

Eric grinned in response. There was nothing innocent in his expression.

"Oh, I fully intend to," the detective promised with enthusiasm. "But it'll be *my* best, not yours." He gave Sean a wide grin just before he left the room.

"Have you two been partners for very long?" January asked the detective as Eric closed the door behind him.

"Under two years," he answered. Remembering what had come before was hard for him and he wasn't about to get into it. Instead, he went on the defensive. "Why would that be important to you?"

"Not important. Just trying to get a handle on the kind of person I'm dealing with," she told Sean, her eyes meeting his.

"Does it make a difference?"

"Sometimes," she allowed. She looked at the little girl who was now working her way through the cookies with gusto. January kept her tone steady. "Children are extremely intuitive about things. You want her to be able to trust you."

"I think I've already established a rapport with her," Sean pointed out, smiling fondly at "Annie." She returned the smile in kind. "It's safe to say that she trusts me."

"It looks that way, but if you don't mind, I'd like to cover all my bases," January told him. "This is all very new to her—and that includes you. In the next few hours, something might come up that could make her change her mind." She knew he couldn't argue with that.

And he didn't.

Sean nodded. "Duly noted. You have any way of finding out her name?"

She decided not to answer his question just yet. "Look, before we go any further, I need you to tell me everything that she might have experienced."

He felt like the social worker was leading him around in circles. "Why should that make any difference, one way or another?"

"So I know what I'm up against," January said simply. "What *she* might be up against," she added. By the expression on his face, she could see that the detective didn't understand what she was telling him. She put it in the simplest terms she could. "I need to be able to get her to trust me and to relate to me. Now tell me what you know."

Sean laughed under his breath. "That's usually my line," he told her.

The corners of her mouth quirked in a fleeting smile. "Welcome to the other side," she said. "Now tell me."

The detective sighed. Just his luck, they had sent a stubborn social worker. But there was no point in wasting any more time going back and forth about this. Besides, it wasn't as if he was revealing any secrets. The story had probably made the news by now.

"There's not much more to tell you than I already

have," Sean said. "There were three men found dead in that warehouse where she was hiding behind some crates. One of the dead men was an informant of mine. I was working with him to bring down a well-connected drug lord."

"What's his name?" she asked. "The guy you were trying to bring down."

Sean debated telling this social worker that she had no "need to know," as the popular phrase went, but then he decided that there was no point in withholding the information from her. "His name is Elias 'Kid' Mercer. Anyway, my informant and two other gang members were found shot dead at the scene."

"And you think this little girl you found there, she saw who killed these men?" January questioned him, looking at the child uncertainly.

Sean ran his hand over the little girl's soft brown hair. He smiled at her as they made eye contact. "I have no way of knowing. That's where you come in."

She frowned as she thought over what he had just said. "You do realize that if word gets out that she witnessed this execution, her life could very well be in danger."

Sean's face clouded over. "You think that hasn't crossed my mind? Look, I don't know the kind of people you're used to dealing with, but I'm not in the habit of endangering children."

The detective had gone from neutral to red-hot in seconds, right before her eyes. It didn't take a degree in psychology to know that she had obviously touched a nerve.

"I didn't mean to imply that that you were," January told him.

In her estimation, he didn't exactly look placated, although the color of his face did return to a normal shade. "Just so you know that I'll do whatever it takes to keep this kid safe."

"Understood," January replied. She made a mental note to ask Stafford's partner about this whole incident if she saw him again. She had a feeling that Stafford wasn't being completely honest with her about what might have happened, and it had something to do with why he was so touchy when she questioned him.

As if realizing how he must have come across, Sean apologized. "Sorry. I didn't mean to snap at you like that. It's been a really long day and I did just lose an informant." He hoped that would satisfy her.

What he didn't say was that finding the informant dead brought back some very bad memories. His former partner, Harry Cartwright, a man he had worked with since he started on the force, lost his wife and daughter while he and Sean were working on a case. The wife and daughter had been collateral damage, a completely unfeeling term for a very personal loss.

The wife and daughter he, Sean, was supposed to have been able to protect but couldn't.

To this day, Sean hadn't been able to shake the guilt that haunted him. He should have been able to save them—should have, but somehow wasn't able to.

After it was all over, Harry didn't leave the force, the way some people had expected him to, but he did leave the department. Left Homicide and transferred over to the Narcotics Division.

The move had hit Sean really hard. Harry had been like a brother to him and not a day went by that he didn't miss working with the man. Sean especially missed the camaraderie that they had shared.

Eric Martinez was a good man, Sean thought, but it just wasn't the same. Because of that, and everything that had gone into what had happened, Sean found himself unable to open up. *Afraid* to open up. Worried that if he did, the same thing might happen again. He knew he couldn't bear that.

"Apology accepted," January was saying to him.

Sean forced himself back to the present.

"Is there anything else I should know?" she asked.

"Nope."

He had answered her a little too quickly, in her opinion. January couldn't shake the feeling that something else was going on here, something she couldn't quite put her finger on.

She had no idea what it might be.

And then again, maybe she was being too suspicious, she thought.

"Okay," January said, nodding and looking back at the little girl. "Let's see if I can find out her name."

"The crime scene investigative unit said they didn't find anything that looked as if it belonged to her, so there was no personal information we could tie to her," Sean said, offering her another nonproductive piece of the puzzle.

"I love a challenge," January murmured with absolutely no enthusiasm. "Let's see what she can tell us."

Coming up to the child, January gently put her hand on the little girl's shoulder to get her attention. The girl looked up at her.

At least there was no fear there, January thought, counting that as a small victory.

With very careful, deliberate movements, January held her breath and began to sign, asking the little girl if she would tell them her name.

Chapter 5

As Sean watched, January's hands almost seemed to fly, forming a number of different positions, which he assumed was the way she asked the little girl for her name. What it did manage to accomplish was to convince the detective that he didn't even know how to *begin* to actually communicate with the little girl whom he had rescued.

When January rested her hands in her lap, he assumed that she had finished the exchange, even though he couldn't make head or tail of it.

"So," Sean asked, "is she willing to tell us her name?"

"She already did," January told him, smiling at the child. "Her name is Maya."

"Maya," he repeated. It had a nice ring to it. "What was the sign for that?" Sean asked.

"There was no isolated sign," she told him. "Maya spelled her name out." Then, for the detective's benefit, she showed him each letter slowly, saying them as she formed them. "M-A-Y-A. Maya."

Sean appeared confounded as he shook his head. "There is no way in the world that I'm going to get the hang of that."

"Well, it's nice of you to want to try," January told him, surprised that the detective said that. "But there's no point for you to attempt to do that if we're going to find her parents."

Sean had his doubts about that. "Provided at least one of them is alive and around," he pointed out. He looked down at Maya's small, heart-shaped face. All sorts of emotions went through him, making him feel outraged and angry that Maya had wound up at the scene of the crime the way she had. "If you ask me, parents who can just lose track of their little girl like that are either dead—or don't deserve to have her in their lives in the first place."

"Hey, don't jump to conclusions yet," January warned him. "In my experience, there are as many reasons for things happening when it involves children as there are children in the system."

He wasn't clear where she was going with this, but he did know how he felt. "Yeah, well, if she were my kid, I wouldn't take my eyes off her. I certainly wouldn't let her run off and play in some abandoned warehouse," Sean said, his emotions bubbling just beneath the surface.

Maya pulled on the edge of his jacket. When Sean looked at her, Maya let go of his jacket so she could talk to him. Keeping her hand open, the little girl tapped her thumb on the side of her forehead. Then, when he didn't respond, she did it again.

Lost, Sean looked over his shoulder at January. "What's she saying?"

"She's asking for her daddy," January told him.

That was when something occurred to the detective. Something unpleasant. Sean exchanged looks with January. "You don't think he was one of the two unknown men who were found dead in the warehouse with my CI, do you?" he asked.

January had another take on the situation. "Could Maya's father have been your contact?"

He thought for a second but realized that he didn't honestly know the answer to that. "I don't think the guy had any kids, but I can't say that for sure. But even if she was his kid, would he have brought her with him, knowing how dangerous it might be?"

January shrugged. "Hey, he's your informant. You would know the answer to that better than I would." And then she pulled back her shoulders, as if she was anticipating something she didn't consider pleasant.

"What are you doing?" Sean asked. In his estimation nothing had changed from a moment ago.

"I'm bracing myself to ask Maya a very jarring, unpleasant question," she told the detective.

Then, before he could say anything one way or the other, January began to sign her question to Maya. This time, for Sean's benefit, January also slowly verbalized it as she signed for Maya.

"Was your dad there in the warehouse today?" she asked the little girl.

Rather than sign something back, looking surprised, Maya moved her head from side to side.

"He wasn't one of the dead men?" Sean asked, a little uncertainly. That was good news in his estimation, but at the same time, it seemed rather unusual to him that the little girl had just wandered into the warehouse by herself.

"Apparently not," January replied.

Maya looked from one adult to the other and then directed a question to January. Because Maya was agitated, her fingers flew even more quickly.

Sean stared, mystified. "What's she saying?"

"Just that she wants her daddy. My guess is that the man is obviously alive somewhere," January said to the detective.

As he watched, she signed something else to Maya and the little girl apparently answered.

"Now what did you ask?" he asked.

"If she saw her dad recently," January answered.

"And?" he prodded.

"She did," the social worker said. Then, as Sean watched, January took the little girl into her arms in an attempt to comfort and soothe her. "Shh, it's going to be all right," January promised her.

He looked at the social worker, puzzled. She had lost him. "I thought you said that Maya can't hear."

"As far as I know, she can't. But a hug is universal.

And Maya responded to it. The words just came out automatically," she added.

"I can see that," Sean said, watching as Maya curled up against January.

Who are you, little girl? How did you get inside that warehouse? Were you lost, or did someone lose you there on purpose? Sean wondered. He really wanted to get to the bottom of this, but it wasn't going to happen tonight.

January glanced in the detective's direction and saw the considering expression on his face. "What are you thinking?"

He wasn't comfortable admitting to having any personal thoughts when it came to his job. He snapped back into work mode.

"That right now, I need to figure out what to do with her for the night." His eyes met January's. "I guess you'd better call your boss, have him send someone to pick her up." And then he smiled down at Maya. Something told him that, in a way, she did understand him even if he couldn't talk to her. "We certainly can't leave her here for the night."

He sounded like he was talking to Maya, January thought, except she knew that *he* knew he couldn't communicate with her in a straightforward manner. Still, January had to admit that she found the whole thing rather touching.

"No, we can't," January agreed. She looked at Maya thoughtfully. "The trouble is, I don't think that there's anyone in our present system who can just take her in. They wouldn't be able to communicate with her. We're shorthanded right now." Although, she thought, that really wasn't anything new.

"Okay," he said, stretching out the word. "So what does that mean, ultimately?" Sean was not quite sure what the social worker was telling him. Where was Maya going to wind up staying tonight? Whether he wanted to or not, Sean found himself being protective of the little girl.

January unconsciously chewed on the inside of her bottom lip, thinking the matter over. "Well, I've got those two weeks coming to me that I have to take."

"Yeah, so you said. The two weeks you told me you were using to go away on vacation," Sean recalled.

"Yes," she confirmed. "I am supposed to be on vacation, but there're no rules about *where* I take my vacation—or how." She could see that she had lost the detective. With effort, she tried to be clearer, even though her own thoughts were jumbled up. "I can temporarily take Maya home with me and foster her. At least until things can be straightened out and you find her parents—or her father, since that's who she's been asking for." She looked at the detective's face to see if she had cleared things up for him.

"Can you do that?" he asked doubtfully. "Just take her in and be her foster parent?" he asked. "Aren't you supposed to be qualified for that or something?"

Sean hated admitting his ignorance about these matters, but in this case, there were huge gaps in his education when it came to knowing things about the foster system. In his defense, he thought, he'd never had a case like this before. The people he dealt with were usually a lot taller—and came with criminal records.

"I do," she said, surprising Sean.

"You're licensed to be a foster parent?" he asked.

January nodded. "Thinking that this might come up as a possibility someday, I became approved to be a foster parent in case the need ever arose. This is the first time that it has," she admitted. "Right now, to complete this temporary arrangement, I just have to get my boss's approval."

"Why don't you call Blackwell, then?" Sean suggested.

They needed to resolve this. He didn't want to see Maya get passed around and possibly traumatized any further. The little girl responded to this woman, and as the social worker had already pointed out, feeling safe could go a long way in getting Maya to trust her.

That also meant that if there was any information to be obtained from her, they would be able to—at least eventually.

But, information or not, Sean had to admit that his first priority was to make sure Maya was safe and *felt* safe. In this case, apparently January was his instrument to help him do just that.

January had crossed to the far end of the room and taken out her phone. It rang five times on the other end before she heard it being picked up.

"Blackwell."

Good, she had caught him. "Hi, Sid, it's January Colton. I know it's late, but there's a problem with the case you wanted me to look into," she told her boss.

"What kind of a problem?" he asked. "And what are you still doing there? I figured that you'd just see what you could find out from the little girl and then have Susan take over."

"Well, that's part of the problem," January admitted, keeping her back to the detective and the little girl. "I sent Susan home."

She could tell by Blackwell's tone that he wasn't exactly overjoyed with her news. "Oh? And why would you do that?"

"Because she was in completely over her head in this case. There wound up being extenuating circumstances. Look, I can fill you in on those in the morning if you'd like," she offered. "Right now, I'm just calling to get your approval."

"My approval. Regarding anything in particular?" her supervisor asked, a partially amused note in his voice. January was one of the best people he had, but she didn't exactly do things by the numbers.

In general, Blackwell was a decent man. January went with that thought, hoping he wouldn't give her an argument about this. In the very short amount of time she had been here, she felt she had managed to forge a bond with Maya. She found herself caring about this child. Her tendency to become personally involved was what more than one person had predicted would wind up being her undoing someday.

But someday wasn't now.

"That little girl the police found in the warehouse, the one that you asked me to communicate with," January began to explain.

"What about her?" Blackwell asked.

January couldn't gauge his mood by his tone, but she pushed ahead anyway. "She needs to be placed with a temporary foster parent until things can get further straightened out."

"And?" Blackwell prodded impatiently when January paused.

"And I'd like to volunteer to be that foster parent," January told him, talking quickly as she added, "I have been vetted and I do have my foster parent license."

She heard Blackwell blow out an annoyed, frustrated breath. "You can't take her on vacation with you, January."

"I know that. I'm not going on vacation, at least, not to that spa and not now. I'll be staying at my town house with Maya instead of going away."

"Maya?" Blackwell asked.

"Maya's the little girl's name. I got her to tell me that," January replied.

"Very good. Progress. So what's her last name?" he asked.

"I haven't gotten that far yet," January admitted. "She's only about five and the police didn't find anything on her or in the area that would give us her last name or her address. But she trusts me, Sid."

"And this is why you want to foster her?" he questioned.

"I know we're shorthanded. The child is deaf and I want her to get special care. Look, Sid, I'm the best hope she has of being reunited with her family which is, after all, our end goal."

"Then there *is* a family?" Blackwell asked, his interest piqued.

"Detective Stafford and I think so," she said, thinking that adding Sean to her side might help tip the scale in her favor. "Maya keeps asking for her father, so I'm hoping that means that he's actually out there somewhere and that we can find him."

Blackwell sighed. "I guess you make a good point. All right, I'm going to grant you temporary custody. But I'm going to have this case monitored by another social worker."

"Of course, Sid. Whatever it takes," January said, relieved that she had won the man over. She saw that Sean was watching her even though her voice was low. She gave him a thumbs-up sign.

"All right. Come in tomorrow, January, and we'll make it official. I'll have you fill out all the paperwork and sign it," her supervisor told her.

January smiled even though she knew he couldn't see her. "I know the drill, Sid."

"Yes, I imagine that you do. One question for you, January," he said before she could terminate the call.

"Yes?" She had no idea what he could think of to ask her. They had already gone over all the important points.

"Don't you know how to relax?" he asked her.

January laughed. "You're the one who sent me here, Sid."

"I was just sending you in as a temporary measure to see what you could ascertain. I didn't realize you were going to use it as another excuse to keep on working."

She didn't want Blackwell pretending to be her conscience. "Goodbye, Sid. I'll see you tomorrow."

"Good," he told her, adding, "I'm looking forward to you telling me how your sisters reacted to this."

Oh Lord, my sisters, January suddenly thought. She had forgotten all about them. She needed to notify them as soon as possible.

This wasn't going to be easy.

"I've got to go, Sid," January said, terminating the call.

"Problem?" Sean asked. He noticed that she was still clutching her cell phone instead of putting it away.

"With my supervisor?" she asked, thinking that was what Sean was referring to. "No, everything's fine there. He signed off on my being Maya's foster mother."

There was more, he could tell. "But…?"

"But?" January asked.

"There's a definite *but* in your voice," Sean told her. "Something's bothering you about this," he guessed. "What is it?"

"Well, it doesn't have anything to do with my supervisor, or with Maya," she said, answering his question slowly.

"But there's someone who isn't going to be happy about this sudden change in your life, even though it is temporary?" the detective guessed.

His immediate thought was that there was either a husband, or at least a significant other, in the picture and that he wasn't going to be happy about this.

"Oh yes," she answered. "Actually, two someones." January thought of Simone and Tatum.

"Two someones?" Sean repeated. "Well, that seems rather ambitious."

"Ambitious?" she asked. She didn't see the connection. "That's rather an odd way to put it."

She was kidding, right? "Well, it isn't every day that I meet a woman who is openly juggling two guys—"

"Two guys?" she echoed, totally confused.

"My mistake, two women," Sean corrected his previous statement. Apparently, his mistake was even bigger than he had thought.

Damn. First time he found himself attracted to someone in longer than he could remember, and it turned out to be someone wouldn't give him a second glance.

"Yes," January acknowledged, wondering what his problem was. "Two women. My sisters, both of whom are going to give me endless grief over my bowing out of our vacation, especially since it was planned around my choice of location."

"Your sisters?" he asked. Why did that piece of information suddenly make him feel happy?

He had no explanation for it, yet there it was.

"Both older and both are going to relish saying, 'I told you so' to each other—and to me." She took a deep breath, still clutching her phone. "I'll be right back," she promised. Then she repeated the message, signing it to Maya, just before she slipped out of the room.

Chapter 6

January looked down at the cell phone in her hand, debating which sister to call. Tatum had always been the more easygoing of the two to deal with, but Simone was the one who had made all the plans and consequently had booked the spa as well as the plane tickets. She knew that telling Simone that she had to bow out because of a work commitment would be the more respectful thing to do.

On the other hand, Tatum wouldn't lecture her and Simone would.

Both sisters loved her, there was no question about that. But Simone was more sharp-tongued and did, on occasion, wind up assuming a superior air when she talked to January.

This is ridiculous, January thought. She decided to

face the music and not put off the inevitable. Because even though she might call Tatum instead of Simone to tell her sister that plans have been changed, somewhere along the line, Simone would call her and let her know that she had "expected this all along."

Just before she dialed Simone, January glanced at the little girl who was the reason she was doing this in the first place.

She was right to do this. There would be other vacation getaways with her sisters, but Maya needed her right now.

Taking a deep breath, January placed her call.

The cell phone on the other end was picked up before the second ring had completed.

"I had a feeling I'd be hearing from you, Jan," Simone said. There was that touch of smugness, January thought, pressing her lips together. "So, what excuse are you going to give us?"

"No excuse, Simone," January replied. "Just the truth."

"And that is?" Simone asked, waiting.

January didn't hesitate. She gave her sister the story straight. "There was a little five-year-old deaf girl found crouching behind some crates in an abandoned warehouse. There were three men found in that same warehouse. They had been killed execution-style. It turns out that I'm the only one here who can communicate with her. So instead of going on vacation, I'm taking Maya—that's her name—home with me so I can try to make her feel safe. Do you have a problem with that?"

For a moment, Simone didn't answer. And then,

using a very different tone, her sister said, "Well, if you put it that way, no. We'll just postpone our vacation and go to that spa some other time—"

"Don't you dare," January cried. She didn't want to ruin everyone's vacation because of something she felt she had to do. "I want you and Tatum to go and have fun for all three of us, do you hear me?"

"While you're getting fitted for your angel wings?" Simone asked.

"No angel wings, Simone," January replied. "I swear, if you saw this little girl's face and thought you could help her, you'd be doing the same thing I am. Now I want you to promise me that you and Tatum are going to be on that plane tomorrow, flying to that spa getaway. Okay? I don't need to feel any more guilty about not being there for this vacation with you than I already do. Now go!"

"Are you sure?" Simone asked her.

"Yes, I'm sure," January assured her sister with feeling.

She heard Simone pretend to sigh. "Okay, we'll do our best. But you're not off the hook by a long shot, little sister," Simone told her. "You owe us a sister getaway, and Tatum and I intend to collect."

"You got it," January promised. "Now I've got to go. But tell Tatum I'm sorry."

"Will do." Simone began to talk quickly before January hung up. "To tell you the truth, I half expected you to call her and not me. Why did you call me?"

So Simone was aware of the way she could sound sometimes, January thought. Apparently, there was hope. "Because it was the right thing to do, Simone," January told her.

"You know, someday those merit badges of yours are really going to start weighing you down, Jan. Take care of yourself—and try to let someone else save the world once in a while," she told her baby sister.

If she argued over Simone's assumption, January knew she wouldn't be able to get off the phone, so she just promised, "Will do."

"Uh-huh," Simone murmured. But before she could say that she knew January was just humoring her, January terminated the call.

January sighed as she shook her head.

"So, did you wind up managing to placate everyone?" Sean asked when she reentered the interview room, putting her cell phone away.

Her head jerked up. January had almost forgotten that he was there. "Yes. For the time being," she told the detective.

Sean had another point he wanted to raise with her. He decided that now was as good a time as any. "Listen, I heard you tell your supervisor, that Blackwell guy," he added for good measure, "that you were planning on taking Maya home with you."

Dealing with Simone had taught her to recognize the signs that she was about to be ambushed. "I am," she answered guardedly.

"Well, to be honest with you," he began, sensing that if he just flat out told her he didn't want her doing something, she was the type who would just roll right over him. "I'm not really very thrilled with that idea."

"I didn't realize that was a requirement, having you thrilled over my taking her into my home," January told the detective.

Okay, maybe he would have better luck being direct, Sean thought. "Look, everything points to this being a dangerous situation."

January stopped him right there. "No kidding, Sherlock," she said. "Isn't that why it was decided that she needed someone to take her in the first place? Because she could be in danger?"

"Yes, but—" Sean began to answer, but got no further than he had the first time.

"Tell me, were you planning on keeping Maya at the police station indefinitely? Because if not," she said, answering her own question before he had a chance to, "then I'm going to take her with me to my town house so I can look after her."

Sean found himself struggling to keep his temper. "Damn but you are one stubborn woman," the detective told January, annoyed.

She met his glare, and for some reason, the expression on his face made her laugh. "You're just finding that out?"

After a moment, Sean's mouth curved. He knew he had one of two choices. He either had to see the humor in this or strangle the woman. Sean decided to see the humor in it, as well as give her credit for having a bigger heart than he had expected.

"No, I kind of figured that out earlier," he admitted. Well, if she was taking Maya home with her, he was going to have to know just where home was. "Look, I'm going to need your address," he began.

January placed her hand over her heart like a Southern belle in an old-fashioned melodrama. "Why, Detective Stafford, this is all just so sudden."

Sean never skipped a beat as he ignored her sarcasm. "So I can have a police car patrol the area every half hour," he told her. He was not about to get sucked into a discussion he had no place taking part in, especially since he found himself reacting more strongly to this woman than he felt was wise on his part. "Unless you have some kind of objections to that," he added.

She surprised him by smiling up into his face. "As a matter of fact, I don't. I appreciate the fact that you are going to be looking out for Maya—and for me," January added after a beat.

He wasn't sure how to respond to that and said the first thing that came to mind. "Yeah, well some things can't be helped."

January suppressed the laugh that rose to her lips, then fluttered her lashes at him. "You mean, like your winning personality?"

He didn't rise to the bait. Instead, he reminded the social worker, "Just remember that you were the one who wanted in on this, Ms. Colton."

January's deportment changed right before his eyes and she became serious as she admitted, "Yes, I know, and I'd do it again in a heartbeat. Let's not lose sight of the fact that Maya is the important person in all of this."

"Not losing sight of that even for a moment," Sean assured her. "Okay, give me your address and I'll see to it that a patrol car will be out in your area, keeping an eye on things. In the meantime, I'm going to escort you home."

"You don't have to do that," January began to tell him. She was perfectly capable of taking herself and Maya home.

Oh no, he wasn't about to get tangled up in that discussion. He was accompanying them to her home and that was the end of it.

"Read my lips," Sean told her, leaning into the social worker to get his point across as he slowly enunciated, "I am going to escort you home."

She nodded. "Okay, then," she replied breezily, reversing direction. "You're escorting me home." January prided herself on knowing when to charge ahead and when to back off.

Taking a notepad from her purse, she quickly wrote down her address for the detective, then handed him the piece of paper.

January pulled up in front of her town house and stopped her vehicle, turning off the ignition. She glanced up into her rearview mirror.

Yup, the detective was still there. True to his word, he had followed her all the way home, staying right behind her.

She got out of her car just as he pulled to a stop.

January glanced toward the back seat. Stafford had managed to procure a child seat for Maya from the lost-and-found department at the police station. She was going to return the seat as soon as she bought one for her car. Right now, she had no idea how long the little girl was going to actually be staying with her.

January considered herself to be a very good driver and she knew that, once upon a time, children just sat anywhere they wanted to in the car. However, accidents did happen no matter how safe a driver might be. She was not about to take any chances, even if there weren't laws on the books about this. It was much better to be safe than sorry. Maya needed to be in a child seat that had seat belts holding it in place.

Glancing at her, she saw that Maya looked as if she had fallen asleep in her seat. So, for now, January left her where she was and turned toward the detective as Sean approached her vehicle.

"Well, this is it," she told Sean, gesturing toward her town house. "I can take it from here."

Sean leaned over and glanced into the car. "She looks asleep."

"I think she is," January confirmed. If Maya was, it might make things easier, at least for now, January reasoned.

He put his hand on the passenger-side door. "I'll carry her in for you."

She didn't want him thinking of her as helpless. "I'm perfectly capable of carrying her in myself, Stafford," she told him.

"I'm sure you are," Sean replied, not about to get into an argument with the woman over this. "Okay, you can carry her in if it makes you feel better—but you bring her into the house *after* I check everything out there and clear all the rooms."

January looked at him, surprised. What he was proposing sounded like something that was on one of those
detective programs that were so popular on TV these
days. "You're kidding, right?" she asked, waiting for
him to say "yes."

"Do I look like I'm kidding?" Sean asked her pointedly.

"To be honest, I really don't know you well enough
to be able to confirm that one way or another," January told him.

"Well, I'm not," Sean answered. "If someone followed you to the police station, they might have wound
up putting two and two together and whoever killed
those three men could very well be waiting inside your
town house."

She had a feeling that there was something he wasn't
telling her, but it was obvious that she wasn't going to
be able to force it out of him right now.

"Are you determined to get me nervous?" January
asked.

"Not determined, no, but when dealing with something like this, it's never a bad idea to be on your guard,"
Sean told her.

Her first instinct was to tell the detective that he was
wasting his time and that he should just go home. But
she had to admit after listening to Sean that there was
a very small part of her that did entertain the possibility that maybe he was right. That maybe someone had
broken into her town house and was waiting for her, for
Maya, actually, to walk in so that any witness to the
murders was eliminated.

So it was for Maya's sake that she agreed to have Sean go inside and clear each room, one by one.

"Go ahead," she told him, gesturing toward the town house. "Have at it." With that, she handed him her house keys.

Meanwhile, Maya had woken up. She instantly began to try to get out of her car seat. Seeing her struggle, January quickly unbuckled the little girl and, taking her into her arms, drew Maya out of the seat. Maya wiggled, as if she was trying to get down. January set her on the ground, thinking that the child would feel more in control of her situation if she could walk into the house under her own power.

Sean waited, the house keys in his hand. Once January reached him, holding Maya by the hand, the detective unlocked the front door. After giving the keys back to January, he slowly drew his gun out, carefully keeping the muzzle pointed away in order not to frighten the little girl.

"All right," he told January. "I want you both to wait right inside the front door until I come back down for you."

"You're actually going to go from one room to another?" January asked him. Part of her thought this was overkill, another part of her thought that perhaps this wasn't enough of a precaution.

"That's what I intend to do," Sean confirmed.

"Be careful," she warned. When he raised his brow in a silent question, January said, "I might have unintentionally left some things scattered around on the floor when I left this morning. I was going to come back and pack for the trip."

"I think I can avoid tripping over scattered luggage and shoes," he told her with an amused smile. "You don't have a dog that's suddenly going to come charging out at me, do you?"

"No, no dog," she answered. "I would have loved to have one," she confided, "but given my lifestyle, it wouldn't have been fair to the dog. I wouldn't be home all that much and I would never have the kind of time for it that the animal would deserve."

"You're that dedicated, huh?" Sean asked as he began to head for the kitchen.

"I don't clock in nine-to-five if that's what you mean," she told him.

"Yeah, I get that," he told her, already putting distance between them as he began to search from one room to another. "We have that in common."

And then he was gone.

Maya stared after him, then looked at January. Making sure she had January's attention, Maya moved her pointer finger from side to side beneath her chin.

"You want to know where he's going?" January asked aloud, knowing Maya was reading her lips. She was a smart little girl, January thought. "He's making sure the house is safe," she told the child as she signed the same message to her.

January felt she should try to make sure that the child had reinforcement and could more easily associate hand signs with spoken words.

She was already thinking beyond tonight, focusing

on the days that were to follow. Whether or not they found the girl's parents, she felt that Maya was going to need to be introduced to the world—and she intended to help with that as much as she could.

She hated the idea of Maya being helpless.

Chapter 7

January saw Maya looking around, her eyes opened extra wide as she appeared to try to take in the entire town house from her vantage point by the front door. January was afraid that the little girl might want to just run off and start to explore the place on her own, but instead, Maya remained at her side, her small fingers wrapped tightly around January's hand.

The little girl might not be impatient, but she definitely couldn't say the same thing for herself, January thought.

What she wanted to do was shout up the stairs to Stafford and get him to tell her how the process was going. But even she knew that shouting was definitely not part of the deal. If she shouted, and there *was* someone on the premises, that would alert the intruder and even, possibly, put Stafford in danger.

Still, there was no denying that she ached to ask the detective if he was done up there, and, if not, how much longer it was going to take until he was.

Instead, January pressed her lips together to keep the words from escaping and sighed.

Because she was learning to become more in tune with Maya, January was aware that the child had turned toward her.

Maya drew her hand from hers and signed, "Where did he go?"

By "he" January assumed the little girl was asking about Stafford. She signed, "He is upstairs, making sure everything is safe."

Maya's furrowed brow vanished after a moment. The answer she'd been given seemed to satisfy the little girl. She took hold of January's hand again, as if that was the position she felt she had to maintain until the detective returned.

They didn't have long to wait.

"All clear," Sean announced, coming back down the stairs. "Doesn't look like anyone's been here," he told January. "And you are probably the neatest 'messy' person I have ever met," he said, referring to the suitcase she had warned him not to trip over.

Sean had found the suitcase standing on the bedroom floor, off to one side and waiting to be opened so that she could begin packing.

"Thank you—I think," January told him a little uncertainly.

His job was officially done, but he could stay in the town house a little longer if it made her feel more secure. He offered as much to her.

Turning around to face January, he said, "I can stick around for a while if you'd like."

She turned him down, just as he'd suspected she would. "Thanks, but we'll be fine, Stafford. It's late and I'd like to get her to bed. You know, try to approximate some semblance of a routine for Maya." January glanced in Maya's direction. "Kids appreciate routines."

"I'll take your word for it. I never had any. Kids, I mean," he added, in case she thought he was referring to having a routine. Those he'd had, one way or another, all of his life.

Even now.

Her eyes crinkled. "Neither have I, but I deal with kids all the time. You get to pick up things," she confided, "even if you don't really realize it."

"I'll keep that in mind."

Time to wrap this up, January thought. "I'll walk you to the door," she volunteered.

"What's your hurry? There's the door." Sean laughed, amused at the less-than-subtle attempt to get him to leave. "I know where the door is, January, but you should lock it after I leave."

She looked at the detective, pretending to widen her eyes. "Thank you. I would have *never* thought of doing that."

"Very funny," he replied drolly, going and then stopping in the doorway. "I'll be back in the morning, Ms. Colton."

The man just didn't let up. "You don't have to check on us," January insisted.

"I'm not checking on you," he informed her. "I'm coming by to take a DNA sample from Maya. I'm going to see if it matches any family member in the database so that we can ultimately get a handle on who she is. Don't forget, there's going to be a police car patrolling the area. During the night, if you hear or see anything that makes you uneasy—anything at all—I want you to call 911. Better yet, here's my card." He took a card out of his pocket and pressed it into her hand. "Call me anytime. I'll be here in a flash."

"Are you planning on sleeping at my doorstep in your car?" She meant it as a joke because of his "flash" comment, but he didn't seem to take it that way.

"Just call my number," Sean instructed again. And then he glanced down at Maya who was still standing beside January, appearing a little lost and more than a little sleepy. "Tell her I'll see her tomorrow morning," he requested.

January signed the message for Maya's benefit. The little girl's fingers immediately flew, responding to the promise from the man who had rescued her.

"What did she say?" Sean asked, looking at January.

"She said she would be right here, waiting for you," January told him.

Sean's smile was warm in response. Somehow, Maya had managed to burrow her way into his heart in an incredibly short amount of time, he thought.

The detective ran his hand fondly over her soft brown

braids, his gesture telling her what he was still unable to on his own.

"Okay, then," he said, turning toward January. "I'll be going," he told her, although he felt a reluctance to do so. His eyes met January's. "I'll see you in the morning," he said, then repeated pointedly, "Lock the door."

"Go, before I give in to my impulse and kick you in the shins," January said, shutting the door behind him.

The second she did, she heard his voice coming from behind the door. "I didn't hear the lock click into place."

"Then you need to have your ears checked," she informed him, raising her voice so he could hear her as she turned the lock.

"Better," Sean acknowledged as he left January's doorstep.

She gave it to the count of five, then turned toward Maya. She found the little girl watching her. There was a question in Maya's expressive brown eyes. It didn't take much for January to guess what was on Maya's mind.

"He's gone home," January signed to the little girl, then added, "He will be back in the morning."

Maya met the assurance with a wide smile followed by a sleepy yawn.

"Okay, time to get you to bed, little one," January said.

When Maya raised and lowered her slender shoulders, January repeated what she had said, this time signing it to Maya. Maya's hands made no response, but January could see that the little girl wasn't about to fight it.

Linking her fingers with Maya's, January took her upstairs. Once she was on the landing, January signed, "I don't have anything for a little girl to wear to bed, but I think that the top half of my two-piece sleepwear might work for you." She offered Maya an encouraging smile. "We'll give that a try."

Maya tilted her head, looking at her. It wasn't hard to figure out what she wanted to know.

January signed the last part of her statement to the girl, then took her by the hand again and led her into the bedroom.

January rummaged through one of her dresser drawers, then another, looking for a particular set of nightclothes. Finally finding what she was looking for, January took the top portion of the outfit out and held it up in front of Maya.

She was rewarded for her efforts with a beatific smile.

You would have thought that that I was holding up Cinderella's ball gown instead of a simple nightshirt top, January thought.

Even so, the little girl looked at her with total, unabashed excitement bubbling wildly just beneath the surface.

"I'd thought you might like it," January told her, then signed the same thing.

She was about to start helping Maya out of her clothes, which were really in pretty bad shape, especially considering the day she had been through.

But she stopped herself in order to sign to the little girl.

"May I help you put on this nightgown?" January asked her.

January felt it was safer that way, since she had no way of knowing if the trauma that Maya had gone through in the warehouse had extended to a physical aspect, as well. The last thing January wanted to do was take a chance of further traumatizing her or bringing up any bad memories for her.

To her relief, the little girl bobbed her head up and down, her eyes appearing to all but shine as she stared at what was, for January, just an ordinary, light pink nightshirt.

With very careful movements, January took off the little girl's dirty jeans and even dirtier T-shirt. She folded each and placed them on the floor beside the bed, leaving them visible as she went on to help Maya slip on the pink nightshirt.

Maya seemed very pleased as she held out the garment from her body, looking down at it. She was even more pleased when she caught sight of herself in it in the wardrobe mirror. She approached the mirror with cautious steps, inspecting herself from all angles.

Her eyes were smiling as she looked up at January. The next moment, she hugged the social worker's arm, beaming at her from ear to ear.

"Glad you like it," January signed to her, then added, "You can keep that if you like. It's yours."

Instead of hugging her arm again, Maya threw her arms around January's waist, gleefully hugging as much of her as she could reach.

January hugged her back. Any second now, she was going to cry, January thought, and she knew that would only confuse Maya. Struggling to regain control over herself, she released the little girl and took hold of her hand instead.

In response to the obvious question in her eyes, January signed to Maya, "Let me take you to your room now."

"My room?" Maya signed back, her small face the picture of wonder and disbelief.

January smiled as she nodded, then signed. "Yes, it's the extra bedroom, but for now, you can think of it as your room."

With that, she led Maya to one of the two guest rooms in the town house. She chose the smaller of the two because that one was located next to her own bedroom instead of down the hall. She didn't want to take a chance on being too far away from the child in case something came up, or Maya became frightened during the night for some reason.

By the look on the little girl's face as they entered the bedroom, in January's estimation, Maya felt as if she had entered paradise.

Pulling back the comforter, January helped the child into the double bed. Like her own bed, this one was made up with 1500 thread count Egyptian cotton sheets and a super-soft comforter. To January there was nothing more important than soft sheets when it came to getting a good night's sleep, and that went for her guests as well as for herself.

She thought, because of everything that had happened today, not to mention that this was all so new and strange to Maya, that it would take the little girl a long time to fall asleep.

January was prepared to sit up with Maya for as long as it took. In her estimation, it would probably be at least an hour, if not more, before the little girl was out.

As she tried to figure out just what to do with herself during this time, January happen to glance at Maya.

She was already fast asleep.

It had taken her all of seven minutes.

January decided to linger for another fifteen, just in case Maya woke up.

But she didn't.

Releasing the breath she had been unconsciously holding off and on for that duration, January carefully slid off the bed.

Even though she logically knew it wasn't necessary, she made her way silently to the bedroom door. Instead of closing it, she made the decision to leave the door open so that if there was any noise during the night, or Maya tried to leave, January would be able to hear that.

This was the same reason January didn't close her own door when she went into her bedroom. Above all, she didn't want Maya feeling as if she was being closed off from anything.

When she got to her room, January decided that she wasn't going to change out of her own outer clothing and into pajamas. She left her clothes on so she would be able to spring up out of bed, ready to handle whatever needed addressing at a moment's notice.

Stafford had done that to her, January thought. Stafford and his story about those dead men in the warehouse. Men who had been executed by other men who could very well be searching to eliminate any witnesses to what they had done.

Men who might suddenly make an appearance in her home. She was a very logical, calm person, but that was in the light of day. There was something about the darkness that coaxed out uneasy, frightening thoughts and they were what she found herself battling right now.

This was ridiculous. She was a grown woman. She wasn't afraid of things that went bump in the night.

Get a grip, January, she ordered herself.

Lying on top of her covers instead of under them, January took a deep breath. She reminded herself that she had just put in a long day and that by all rights, she should have been exhausted, not coming up with scary, outlandish scenarios.

"Close your eyes, January. You need your rest," she insisted. "And you're going to need your rest so you can face tomorrow without sleepwalking. You can do this. Close your eyes and take a deep breath. In, out. In, out," she repeated as she forced herself to close her eyes.

After a while, she could feel herself relaxing, one tight muscle at a time. It took a few more minutes, but she had almost convinced herself that she was actually drifting off to sleep.

Curling up on her side, January buried her face against her pillow. Her self-hypnosis began working. She slipped into a dreamlike state.

Before long, she was one step removed from actual sleep.

The strange screeching noise penetrated the wall of sleep she had begun to construct around herself.

At first, she thought it was all part of her waking-dream state.

But when the screech-like moan came again, January realized that it wasn't a dream, or even some trapped animal, which had been her next thought.

Maya!

Bolting upright, January's feet hit the floor before she even realized what she was doing.

The next second, she was racing to the room next to hers.

She found Maya cringing in the bed, her eyes shut as she went on whimpering, making those awful noises that had woken January up.

January lost no time scooping Maya up into her arms.

Still asleep, her eyes squeezed shut, Maya began to beat her fists against January, crying and desperate to break away.

But January went on holding her, rocking her body and doing her best to soothe the little girl until Maya finally stopped making those strange, frightened noises. Her eyes suddenly flew open.

They were filled with terror.

When she finally became conscious—and realized where she actually was—Maya stopped hitting January. Instead of making that unearthly sound, the little girl began to sob, her body shaking. Her small arms tightened around January, as if she was trying to draw strength from her.

"It's okay," January said in a soothing voice, even though she knew the little girl couldn't hear her. She could only hope that on some level, Maya could "feel" the words she was saying to her and that by their very utterance, they would wind up comforting her.

Or at least they would wind up negating the effects of Maya's nightmare or whatever it was that had wound up terrifying her.

"I bet that there are a lot of things you've seen and gone through that have scared you," January whispered against Maya's hair. "But I'm right here and I'm going to protect you, I promise."

Chapter 8

It took January a while before she could get the girl to calm down. Once Maya finally did, January tried to get her to talk about her nightmare.

But instead of signing an answer, or attempting to elaborate, Maya just vigorously shook her head.

January knew better than to push.

"You'll tell me in your own time," she signed to Maya, offering a smile.

The little girl continued to seem pensive. And then, a few minutes later, Maya wanted to know when her daddy was coming to get her. Signing, she repeated the question to January not once, but several times. Each time she did, she appeared to grow more agitated when January told her she didn't know.

January tried another approach. "Maybe I can call

him for you. What's your daddy's last name?" she signed. As intelligent as Maya seemed to be, the little girl had no answer for her. All she did was to once again make the sign for daddy.

"Okay," January murmured, resigned, "No last name. Do you know his first name?" she signed, trying again and hoping that this might be the start of solving this particular puzzle.

Maya looked up at her and signed, "Daddy," in response.

As a last-ditch approach, January asked the little girl if she knew her address. Just as she had expected, Maya had no answer for that, either.

This was getting her nowhere. Maybe she could make a little headway with Maya in the morning. At least she could hope, she thought, mentally crossing her fingers. Right now she was fresh out of ideas and too tired to try to come up with any new approaches.

Rather than leave the little girl alone in the guest room again, this time January lay down next to her, thinking that having her close by would somehow comfort Maya.

She was pleased to have guessed right. The little girl began to relax.

Maya was asleep within a few minutes.

This time, January wasn't all that far behind her. Falling asleep with her arm loosely tucked around Maya's waist, January remained that way for what was left of the night.

However, when she woke up, January hardly felt as if she had slept at all. For half a second, she thought she was late. She still needed to pack for her flight to the spa getaway with her sisters.

She had no sooner thought that than she remembered. She'd had Simone cancel those reservations for her so that she could spend her vacation with Maya until the little girl's parents, or at least someone in her family, could be located.

January felt no regret over her canceled plans, only a sense of anxiety that maybe they wouldn't be able to locate *any* family members. That would mean there wouldn't be anyone to take Maya in.

January sighed, trying to blink the sleep out of her eyes. "Well, aren't you just the ray of sunshine?" she asked herself in a mocking tone.

She stretched, feeling less than fresh. Her body protested. But this wasn't the first time she had deliberately gone to sleep in her clothes or in an awkward position. She had stayed up all night in a hospital chair recently, keeping vigil. It had been at the bedside of a little boy who had been badly abused by his stepfather while his mother had done nothing to step in or try to save him. The boy, Daniel, had been rescued by a neighbor who had heard his screams. Because of internal bleeding, Daniel wound up needing surgery, and because she had been assigned to his case at the last minute, she had stayed with the boy while he recovered.

That was how she had wound up sleeping in a chair next to his bedside. She hadn't wanted the nine-year-old waking up to feel as if he had been abandoned and was all alone.

The only difference between the cases, she thought,

other than the gender of the children, was that Daniel could hear her when she spoke. Getting Maya to understand her took a little extra effort. She had also known more about the boy and his background than she did about Maya.

Patience, she told herself. *Patience*.

Quietly slipping off the bed, January went into the bathroom. She threw some cold water in her face in an effort to try to feel human again.

When she came out, January found Maya sitting up in bed, obviously watching for her to reenter the bedroom.

"Hi, sleepyhead," January signed, then asked, "Are you hungry?"

Maya's face lit up in response and she nodded her head.

"Good, let's get some breakfast," January signed, then took Maya's hand, getting her to stand up. "After that," she continued, "we'll find you something clean to wear."

Maya looked over toward where her dirty jeans and T-shirt were lying folded on the floor. She pointed to the clothing.

"Something cleaner," January emphasized.

With that, she put her hand out to Maya again, waiting for her to take it. Maya immediately grasped it, reaffirming that the little girl trusted her. January gave her a quick hug, then they went downstairs.

Once in the kitchen, January put on the coffee. In all the excitement the previous night she had completely forgotten to do that. Her morning didn't start until she had the dark liquid coursing through her veins.

As the coffee maker began to make noise, going through its paces, January opened the refrigerator door to see what she could offer Maya for breakfast. Because, until last night, she had been scheduled to leave on vacation today, she purposely hadn't restocked certain items. If things had gone according to plan, she would have been away for almost two weeks. She hadn't wanted her refrigerator filled with things going bad in that time.

Consequently, although her supply of coffee was as healthy as it always had been, the rest of the food was limited: eggs—two—bread—two slices—and as for meat, she had one hamburger patty on the shelf in case she'd been feeling particularly hungry before she left for the airport.

Beyond that, there was nothing.

"Looks like the cupboard is practically bare," January murmured as she rummaged through the crisper drawers at the bottom of the refrigerator.

As she concluded the inventory, she felt Maya tugging on her sleeve. When she glanced at the girl, Maya raised her hands, indicating that she didn't understand what January had just said.

"Sorry," January signed, then went on to repeat it, this time signing it to Maya.

As if to disprove what January had just said about the cupboard being bare, the little girl opened the refrigerator door farther and proceeded to point to the two eggs, the all but depleted bag of bread, and the lone hamburger patty on a plate.

"You're right," January signed back with a laugh. "It's not really bare. Where are my eyes?"

In response to that, Maya tugged January down to her level, then with a surprisingly gentle touch, she pointed first to one of January's eyes and then the other.

January tried not to laugh as she said, "My mistake again."

Straightening up, January went on to make Maya two scrambled eggs along with two slices of toast. When she put the meal on a plate in front of Maya, the little girl lost no time starting to eat. But then Maya abruptly stopped and looked up. Putting down her fork, she signed, "What about you?"

The very act tugged at January's heart. Not everyone, child or adult, was that thoughtful.

"I'll eat later," January said as she signed the answer.

Maya shook her head, as if she didn't believe her. Taking a bread plate that was on the side of the table, she divided what was left of her breakfast so that January could have something to eat, too.

"You've got a good heart," January told her quietly. "If your parents *are* alive, I know they've got to be looking for you. I hope Stafford can find them."

Rather than asking for her to sign what she had just said, Maya looked at her with a wide smile. January felt that she seemed to understand.

After breakfast was over and the dishes cleared, January took Maya upstairs again to find her something to wear. Rummaging through her closet, January found a pretty peasant blouse that, with the proper tie acting as a cinch around her waist, became a slightly large pink peasant dress on the little girl.

"There, you look lovely," January signed, pleased with her handiwork. "And just in time, too." Her cell phone was ringing.

January was rarely without her phone and it was a good thing, too, she thought as she looked at the name on the screen.

Sean Stafford.

"Looks like your admirer is going to be here." January signed as much to Maya, ready to explain what she meant by that term. But she didn't have to. The little girl seemed to know who January meant, and she immediately grew excited. "Ah, so much for playing hard to get." January laughed.

When Maya asked her what she had just said, January signed, "Never mind," and gestured for the little girl to follow her downstairs.

Reaching the bottom of the steps, January answered her phone and asked, "So, when are you getting here?"

"Try now," Sean told her. "I'm standing on your front step."

Well, that certainly wasn't much warning. "And what if I wasn't dressed?" she asked.

She heard a warm chuckle rumbling against her ear. January pressed her lips together. She had obviously said something that struck him as funny.

"I don't mind," he told her cavalierly.

"Very big of you," January commented as she walked over to the front door. She hung up, opened the two locks and turned the doorknob.

"I try to be easygoing," Sean said just as she opened the door. His eyes met hers a second before he walked into the house. "I take it you didn't get much sleep last night."

"What makes you say that?" she asked. She closed the door behind the detective and then proceeded to flip the locks as he looked at her. She wasn't about to give him the satisfaction of reminding her to lock the door—again.

"Oh, I don't know. Maybe because you don't exactly look all that rested," he answered. "Since you didn't call me last night or this morning, I'm assuming that nothing out of the ordinary happened here."

"Other than Maya having nightmares," she said, sensing he would want to know about that. "No."

By now Maya had thrown her arms around Sean, greeting him affectionately.

"Hi, little one." He smiled at her as he ran one hand over her curls. Looking in January's direction, he asked, "She had nightmares?"

She could see that he was concerned. "Given the way you found her, could you expect anything less?"

"Taking what happened into consideration, I don't think I would have been able to fall asleep if I were her," Sean said.

"Well, luckily, she did for a while—until the nightmares woke her up."

"And you, did you get any sleep?" he asked.

She shrugged. "Me, not so much. At least it didn't feel like I did." Then, uncomfortable talking about herself, she changed the subject. "If you're hungry," she continued, leading him into the kitchen, "I can offer you a hamburger patty or coffee."

"Ah, a regular feast," he commented, his lips quirking to form an amused smile.

"My refrigerator was expecting me to go on vacation," January told him. "I didn't think it was smart to leave a full refrigerator if I wasn't going to be home."

Opening the refrigerator door, Sean looked around the shelves. Except for a barren plate and a couple of empty wrappers that had fallen off and been overlooked, the shelves were all but empty.

"I'd say mission accomplished," he concluded. Closing the door again, the detective turned to her. "I thought you were kidding."

"Well, let that be a lesson to you. I never kid about food," January said, deadpan.

Sean nodded his head. "So I see. After I take that DNA sample I came for and drop it off at the lab, I can go shopping for you and this lovely little lady dressed in pink," he said, volunteering his services as he smiled at Maya.

January signed what the detective said, and Maya responded by covering her mouth and giggling.

"You flattered her," January explained, then added, "and we can do our own shopping, thank you. As a matter of fact, I intend to make going grocery shopping our little project for the day. I get the feeling that she doesn't get to do a lot of normal, everyday things.

"By the way, you should know that she asked for her father again. Several times, actually. Most adamantly right after she woke up from that nightmare she had," she told Sean.

He looked at the DNA kit he had brought with him,

which, in essence, was a large cotton swab. "Well, let's see if we can narrow the playing field and find her daddy for her—and her mommy, too, if the woman is anywhere in the picture."

"I get the feeling that Maya would be asking for Mommy if that were the case. I'm guessing that Mommy either left or is dead," January speculated.

"You're probably right," Sean agreed, "but until we have confirmation one way or another, let's just assume that she is somewhere out there."

"Fine by me," January agreed. She wanted to move this along. "For now, why don't you focus on getting that DNA sample from Maya so the lab can run the test on it? You'll tell them to put a rush on it, right?"

He surprised her by laughing. "You obviously haven't had all that much contact with police labs, have you? I'll make it easy for you," Sean told her. "The lab techs all plead overwork."

"You can't flex your muscles or bat your lashes or whatever it takes to get the tech to respond and put you at the head of the list?" she asked.

Her inexperience in this matter really amused Sean. "Well, it's obvious that someone's been watching way too many TV crime procedurals."

"I don't have time to watch procedurals," she informed him with a touch of indignation. "I'm way too busy dealing with the real world and kids who have been abandoned or abused by people who were supposed to love and care for them. And, if you must know, I also think that you have a way about you that gets people to do whatever you want them to. I'm just telling you to use your 'special power' so that if Maya's father or mother is alive, we get to unite them as quickly as possible."

Intrigued and more than a little fascinated, Sean cocked his head and asked whimsically, "Anything else you'd like me to do while you're making requests?"

An answer rose to her lips, but she wasn't about to make the mistake of actually giving voice to it. Although, admittedly, there was a part of her that would have loved to find out what Sean's mouth would feel like pressed against hers.

Given that there was a child in the room, not to mention that giving in to the impulse would create a host of other complications, she couldn't actually *say* that to the detective—or even have him suspect it.

So, instead, January merely said, "No, that'll do for now."

"Okay, then, why don't we go somewhere comfortable so I can get that sample we need from this little princess?" he asked, smiling at Maya.

"Or we could just do it in the kitchen," January suggested.

"Sounds good. Tell Maya for me," he requested, turning his attention back to the little girl.

January did as he asked, signing to the little girl exactly what the detective was going to do.

After looking uncertain at first, Maya finally sat back down at the table and opened her small mouth.

Chapter 9

When Sean took the long cheek swab out of its plastic wrapper, Maya's eyes grew huge and she scooted back on her chair, clutching at the seat, as if that was enough to get her out of the detective's reach. She also closed her mouth—tight.

January immediately signed, telling the little girl that it was all right.

Maya shook her head. "No, it's not," Maya signed back. "I will choke on the stick if he pushes it into my throat."

Before January could explain that all the detective was going to do was rub the swab against the inside of her cheek, Sean had taken out a second swab. He had brought the swab with him just in case something happened to the first one.

Getting Maya's attention, Sean elaborately un-wrapped the swab, then went on to use it on himself to demonstrate to the little girl just how quick, painless and harmless the whole process was. He rubbed the swab on the inside of his cheek, took the stick out and proceeded to hold it up for her inspection.

Glancing at January, he asked, "How do you sign *done?*"

Raising both hands, January moved them from the area at the top of her shoulders down midway to her waist as if she was trying to brush off sparkles.

Flashing him a smile, she declared, "Done."

"Okay." Mimicking the movement, he looked at Maya as he did it, then said, "Done."

Very slowly, a small, shy smile bloomed on Maya's heart-shaped face. The next moment, she tilted her head back and opened her mouth. Everything about her body language told the detective she was ready for this to happen.

"Very brave," he told Maya, his eyes shining with approval.

Out of the corner of his eye, he saw January sign his spoken sentiment to the little girl.

Sean swabbed the inside of her right cheek quickly, then held up the long stick he had used for her inspec-tion. When she nodded her head, satisfied, he felt it was safe to proceed.

With the same sort of elaborate movements he had used with his own swab, Sean took the swab he had just used on Maya and placed in the plastic bag, pressed the edges on either side together, locking the bag, and then put that in a paper bag.

January had watched the whole thing without saying a word. She was very impressed, not just with his patience, but with the amount and degree of empathy that the detective had displayed.

"They teach you that at the police station?" she asked him when he had finished taking the sample.

"Some things can't be taught," he told her with a simple smile.

"You mean like putting pressure on tab techs?" she asked him.

He snorted, shaking his head. "You just don't stop, do you?"

She held up her hands. "I have no idea what you're talking about," she answered, giving him an innocent look. And then she gave credit where it was due. "But you're very good with her. You put her at ease."

His eyes met January's, and just for the briefest second, he caught himself entertaining thoughts that had no business being in his head.

"Too bad I can't seem to do that with her handler," Sean responded, just as he banished the thought from his head.

"There's no need to put me at ease," she told him. "I work best when I'm on the edge." She cleared her throat before he could draw her in any further with those magnetic bright-green eyes of his. "Now, if you've finished that coffee I poured for you, my suggestion is that you get yourself to that lab posthaste," she told him, pointing at the bag with the swab in it.

"What about my offer?" Sean asked. When January looked at him quizzically, he elaborated. "You know, the offer to go grocery shopping for you and fill your refrigerator."

Hadn't he paid attention to what she had said to him? "How long have you had this problem retaining things?" she asked. Before he could ask her what she was talking about, January told him. "I said that Maya and I were going to make a day of it, going food shopping and just doing something normal. I thought it would be good for her."

He wasn't keen on her being out there with Maya, even in broad daylight. He would definitely feel better if he—or at least a patrol officer—was with her.

"And if I asked you to wait until I got back and could go with you?" he asked.

She didn't like being viewed as helpless. "Sorry, Stafford. No can do."

Two could play this stubborn game, he thought. "All right, then I'm attaching a plainclothes officer to follow you."

She frowned, but she supposed she could see his reasoning. "All right, as long as he puts enough distance between him and us not to spook Maya. She's been through enough," January stressed.

"No argument, but I don't want her possibly having to go through even more," Sean pointed out, "which means keeping her safe."

January rolled what he said over in her head. The way January saw it, her choices were between bad and worse. She pressed her lips together, looking at the detective. Sean represented the lesser of two evils and, happily, he didn't scare Maya. She actually responded to him.

"All right," January said with a sigh, surrendering. "You win."

The corners of his mouth curved. "And what is it that I win?" he asked, taking the DNA sample with him to the door.

He was really going to make her say it, she thought, surprised.

Looking at his expression, she realized that he was. With another sigh, she said through clenched teeth, "Maya and I will wait until you get back before going grocery shopping."

Sean nodded his head. "I take it back," he told her.

January stared at him, confused. She didn't understand. "Take what back?"

Sean's smile widened. "What I was thinking about you."

Which meant, she thought, that initially it had been something less than flattering. "Careful, Detective. I'm not as harmless as I look," January warned, making a fist at her side for emphasis.

They were back, those thoughts about her that he had absolutely no business entertaining in the present atmosphere.

With effort, Sean managed to shut them down.

Again.

He looked at her intently. "Oh, I know you're not," he quietly agreed.

January had no idea what he meant by that, but his

tone was way too sexy to be construed as being harmless. It took her a moment to find her tongue. Her mouth felt far too dry.

"You'd better get going," she told Sean. Belatedly, she began to walk him to the door.

Maya was directly behind them, shadowing their every move.

"If you're going to be any use to us, you need to hurry back as soon as possible," January told him.

"You got it. Be back as soon as I can," Sean said, opening the door. But he paused just before he pulled it shut behind him. "You are going to stay put, right?"

"Absolutely." She gave him a quick salute. "Scout's honor."

Sean turned to look at her dubiously. "You were a Girl Scout?" he asked.

The way her eyes sparkled when she smiled at him, Sean didn't know if she was being serious or pulling his leg.

"I've got the merit badges to prove it," she responded cheerfully.

He decided that, for the sake of expediency, he had no choice but to believe her. "All right, I'll take you at your word." He paused to wave goodbye to Maya and then he was gone.

The little girl looked up at January, then signed a question.

"Yes," January assured her, signing. "He's coming back."

Her statement drew a huge smile in response. It didn't take much to figure out what was going on in

Maya's head. "You, little girl, have a serious case of hero worship going on," January murmured under her breath.

January happened to glance down at her clothes and realized that she still hadn't changed them, not since yesterday morning. Well, if nothing else, she could use this down time to put on a fresh outfit, she consoled herself.

"Come with me," she signed to Maya.

"To where?" the little girl signed back, cocking her head.

"Definitely not a trusting soul," the social worker in her decided. Maybe that was a good thing.

"To my room," she signed, then smiled as she added, "So I can put on something that doesn't look as if I slept in it."

"But you did," Maya signed.

January laughed, then pointed to the stairs, raising her hand from the bottom step to the top of the landing.

Maya lost no time in running up the stairs, as if she thought it was a race of some sort.

With that in mind, January took her time going up, sensing that winning something as insignificant as getting to the top of the stairs first was somehow important to Maya. She had a feeling that gratification was not something that happened often for the little girl.

So, when January did reach the top of the stairs, she inclined her head toward Maya, as if she was conceding the race.

"You win," she signed. "I'll win next time."

Maya signed back, "Maybe," and smiled from ear to ear.

There was a touch of humbleness about Maya, January thought, warmed.

She put her arm around the girl's shoulders and guided Maya into her bedroom so January could pick out something to wear for this proposed grocery shopping field trip.

A couple of minutes passed before she realized that she was looking over the outfits hanging in her closet with a critical eye. The clothes were all very serviceable, of course. She had worn all of them to work at one time or another. But even so, for some reason, January caught herself dismissing each and every one.

What was she doing? *This isn't a date*, January silently insisted, annoyed with herself and where her thoughts were. She was just picking out something to wear while she was grocery shopping, for heaven's sake. Any one of the outfits she had looked at would do as long as it covered all the essential parts. And they all did.

With that in mind, she took out a pair of gray slacks and a turquoise, long-sleeved V-neck pullover. Because Maya was there on the bed, watching her intently, January held up her choice for the little girl to view, wanting Maya to feel as if she was an active part of this whole process.

Maya beamed and nodded her approval.

"Okay, I'll just go and put this on," January signed, stepping into the bathroom.

But before she could close the door so she could change out of what she was wearing and put on the slacks and top, Maya had squeezed herself into the room right behind her. The little girl proceeded to sit down, cross-legged, on the tile floor.

And then she looked up, waiting.

January's natural inclination was to tell the girl to wait for her in the bedroom until she had finished changing. But again she sensed that Maya felt better if she stayed close to her.

For better or worse, it seemed that the girl had formed an attachment to her as well as to the detective—or maybe she was being substituted for Detective Stafford until he could return. Either way, January wasn't about to make Maya feel as if she was being abandoned or rejected. Not even if the gesture was perpetuated by something as small and insignificant as closing the bathroom door to separate them.

So, with Maya sitting right there on the floor, January hurried out of the outfit she had been wearing since the previous morning and put on the slacks and top that she had picked out today. The available space in the bathroom made the change of clothing tricky for her, but January managed.

After pulling a hairbrush through her long blond hair so it didn't look like something the wind had just blown in, January put on some lipstick and turned toward Maya.

"All ready. Let's go," she signed to Maya as she put a hand out to her.

There was a look of utter gratitude on the small, angelic face that January couldn't begin to describe.

Maya curled her small hand around hers. The warmth

pulsating in January's chest spread out soft, tender fingers that reached throughout every part of her.

It was becoming a very familiar feeling for her.

"Okay," January said to herself once they reached the bottom of the stairs again. "Now all we have to do is wait for Detective Stafford to show up here. But he better hurry," she murmured, "or you and I are going to fly the coop."

Maya looked at her and shook her head, indicating that she didn't understand. She had been trying very hard to read lips, January realized, but her efforts weren't proving all that fruitful.

"Sorry," January signed, then went on to sign to Maya roughly what she had murmured to herself.

With a nod of her head to indicate that she understood, Maya surprised January by walking up to the front door. She positioned herself by one of the windows that framed the upper portion of the door. For all intents and purposes, she looked as if she was standing guard there.

"Looks like you have got yourself a groupie, Stafford," January said under her breath to the absent homicide detective.

Maya's sweet, unassuming behavior made January think about the girl's parents again, or at least about the daddy she kept asking after.

Why weren't those people combing the streets, looking for her? Or more to the point, why hadn't there been a missing person report filed on Maya, offering a reward and searching for her whereabouts the moment they realized she was gone?

"If you were my little girl, Maya," she said to the child's back, "I would be out there, searching and leaving no stone unturned until I found you."

She saw Maya's back suddenly grow rigid and the little girl all but stood at attention.

"What do you see?" January asked as she made a beeline for the door. And then she remembered that Maya had been watching through the glass that framed either side of the door. That way, she would have been able to see Stafford coming up the front walk.

The next moment, as she heard the doorbell, January knew her conjecture had to be right.

"Speak of the devil," she said as she opened the front door.

"Oh, were you speaking of the devil?" Sean asked, walking in.

"No, but you're the next best thing," January said, even as Maya threw her arms around him.

Sean laughed as he scooped the little girl up and gave her a quick, warm hug. "Hi, princess, did you miss me?"

Maya seemed to get the general gist of what he was asking without having January sign what Sean had said.

Setting the girl back down on the ground, the detective looked at January. "Ready to go?"

"We've been ready since you left," she told him.

He didn't know if she was being sarcastic or critical, but he let it go. Glancing at January's new attire as he held the door open for her and Maya, he said, "Nice outfit," then closed the door behind them.

Chapter 10

"Was that sarcasm?" January asked as she walked out holding Maya's hand.

"No. Why?" he asked. "Haven't you ever been on the receiving end of a compliment before?"

"Yes, of course. But when it comes to you, I'm not exactly sure if you're being on the level or putting me on."

"I promise, you'll know when I'm not being on the level," he told her as he watched January go directly to her vehicle. He didn't understand. "And why are you opening up your car? We're going to go to the store in mine."

January stood her ground, making no move to comply. "That car seat we got from the police station is already installed in my car. Why go through all the trouble of uncoupling it, putting it into your vehicle and making sure it is all secured there?" she asked. "Seems like an awful lot of trouble to go through for the same results. Besides, I already know the way to my market. I might as well drive there instead of giving you the directions."

He wasn't entirely sure what she was telling him. "I wasn't planning on driving blindly around," he told January. "I was going to ask you how to get there. I'm sure you're very good at telling people where to go."

She congratulated herself on not responding to his comment. "Well, now you don't have to ask," she said, smiling brightly at him. Perhaps a little *too* brightly, she conceded, but it was better than snapping at him. "Just buckle up and enjoy the ride there."

He frowned as he waited for her to secure Maya in the car seat in the back. "Tell me, is everything always a debate with you?" he asked, addressing the back of her head as she worked.

January smiled as she glanced at the detective over her shoulder. "Not if you go along with whatever I tell you. You know, it takes two for a debate."

"Yeah, it does," Sean agreed, looking at her pointedly.

She had a feeling that they were standing on the edge of a possible blowout, or at least what could turn into a very nasty argument. Taking a breath, she decided to retreat. There was nothing to be gained by locking horns anyway.

"Did they by any chance tell you how long you'll

have to wait before they can give you Maya's DNA results?"

That hadn't taken her long to get to, he thought. Sean gave her the outside estimate that he'd been given, even though he knew it could be done faster. "Forty-eight hours," he said.

"That long?" she asked, turning around to look at him. "And you couldn't get them to try to speed things up?"

"Sorry," he deadpanned, winking at Maya just before he got into the front passenger seat. The little girl looked very pleased even though she had no idea what was going on. "The lab tech I talked to told me that the department's magic wand was out getting repaired."

January frowned as she got into the front seat behind the steering wheel. She resented the detective's flippant response.

And she wasn't about to back off, at least, not yet. "It's just that I remember hearing that a top lab can get results to a test in about twenty-four hours—or less," she told the detective.

"Yeah," he agreed, seeing no reason to contest that. "If they don't have anything else waiting to be processed. Unfortunately, this is Chicago," he said with emphasis.

It wasn't as if this was the heart of the city, she thought. "A *suburb* of Chicago," January stressed, buckling up.

"Still not exactly a sleepy little town," Sean answered. "Look, I'm as anxious as you are to get an answer and find Maya's parents—*if* they're still alive and *if* they're in the DNA database."

"And you're sure that her father wasn't one of the dead men in the warehouse?" she asked. They had already gone over this once, but, January thought, it wasn't exactly inconceivable to think that a mistake might have been made in the identification.

"He wasn't," Sean confirmed. "The crime scene investigators identified all three of them. They were all drug dealers, including my source. They were all trying to get out of the life and start new somewhere else by giving me the information I needed. Coincidentally, neither of the other two men who were killed at the scene was the guy I was looking to bring down, either."

He hadn't mentioned this before. "And who is that— or is that one of those 'need to know' things that I have always found to be so damn infuriating?" January asked him with feeling.

He noticed that her hands were gripping the steering wheel a little more tightly than he would have expected. This being kept out of the loop really bothered her, he thought.

"Considering that you've gotten pulled into this, I suppose I can tell you," Sean said. He kept his expression neutral so as not to somehow convey to Maya that something was amiss. "I'm trying to bring down a well-connected criminal in this drug cartel."

"What's his name?" she asked again.

"Elias Mercer. He goes by 'Kid' Mercer because the guy has this baby face. It throws people off because, trust me, there's nothing kid-like about the man," Sean told her grimly. "I think either he or one of his people killed those three men at the warehouse to keep them from talking to the authorities about what they knew about Mercer's operation."

He glanced over his shoulder at Maya. Now there was total innocence, he couldn't help thinking. "That's also why I'm worried about the princess here. Most likely she didn't see anything. And I know she certainly didn't hear anything, but if Mercer suspects that she might have—even if it wasn't possible—a man like that wouldn't think twice about having Maya eliminated. For a man like that, there is no age restriction," he told January.

He saw the social worker turn pale. "Look, I'm not trying to scare you," the detective began.

"Too late," she informed him. But she knew she couldn't afford to just stick her head in the sand. These were dangerous people who had killed those men in the warehouse. "But better forewarned than blindsided," she said philosophically. January stole a glance at Sean. "You're sure that patrol car you told me about is going to be passing by my house on a regular basis?" It wasn't herself she was worried about. She was thinking of Maya.

Sean didn't hesitate. "Absolutely."

She blew out a breath, then forced a smile to her lips. "Well, that's good enough for me."

The next minute, she turned a corner and drove into a large parking lot, looking for a space near the front of one of Oak Lawn's larger grocery stores.

"Okay," January announced. "We're here."

Then, pulling up the handbrake and turning off the ignition, she turned toward Maya and signed what she had just said to Sean. That they had arrived at their destination.

Maya peered out her window, seeming a little uncertain at the sight of the store. Sean saw her expression and wondered if she was afraid or if this was just new to her. In any case, he wanted to set her mind at ease.

"Why don't I get her out of her seat?" he suggested to January.

He really was turning out to be a very thoughtful person, January thought. "I think that might be a good idea," she responded, adding, "It's obvious that Maya feels safe with you."

Sean grinned at the little girl. "Well, she has to be the smallest damsel in distress I've ever worked with to feel that way," he told January. There was a touch of humor in his voice.

Just before they entered the store, January grabbed a cart, then brought it over to Sean. She assumed he would deposit Maya in the seat so that they could get around the store faster, thereby making shopping easier all around. She was certain that he wanted to get this over with as quickly as possible.

But Sean surprised her with another idea. "Maybe Maya would like to push the cart instead of sitting in it?" he told January.

"I just thought it would be easier for her—and us," January said.

"Yeah, but maybe easier is not the way to go," Sean

said. "I've got a feeling that Maya would be happier if she was being challenged."

"She's a little girl," January pointed out.

"Little girls need challenges if they're going to grow up to be competent, smart big girls, and more importantly, competent, smart young women," Sean concluded.

For a second, January was speechless. The detective's answers and insight really intrigued her. There was apparently a lot more to this man than was obvious at first.

January laughed softly. "I thought I was the social worker," she said.

"Oh, you are," Sean readily agreed. "I'm just here to offer advice and to provide protection."

"I thought you were here to show off your shopping prowess," she teased.

"That's just a bonus," Sean cracked. Standing behind Maya to help her with the cart if it turned out to be too unwieldy, he asked January, "Okay, where to first?"

"Why don't we start at the meat department and then work our way out to the other aisles?" she suggested, signing her words to Maya as she said them out loud for the detective's benefit.

Maya looked as if she was getting all excited and was more than ready to begin this adventure with the people she apparently viewed as her two new best friends. The little girl wrapped her hands around the cart's handle, looking very intense. She made January think of a racehorse at the starting gate, pawing at the ground and poised to react the moment she heard the sound of the starter's pistol.

January observed Maya as the little girl made her way down the aisle, with January walking on one side of the cart and the police detective walking on the other. What impressed her most was that Maya didn't act as if she was Alice in Wonderland. She behaved as if being in a grocery store of this caliber was extremely familiar to her.

"You know, I think Maya might know this neighborhood," January speculated as she looked at Sean over Maya's head. "At least, that's my working theory."

"Given that theory, it broadens my search base," Sean told her, and then he nodded toward Maya. "Why don't you ask her what she would like to eat tonight?" he suggested.

She didn't quite follow him. "Why? You think what she wants to eat will tell us something about her?"

Where had that come from? "I think that'll tell you what she likes to eat so you can make it for her and wind up with a contented little girl on your hands. A contented kid tends to be more cooperative."

Sean had managed to impress her again. "You know, if you ever feel like leaving the police force, there might be a spot for you in social services," January told him.

"Sorry, but dealing with all those kids without families, or with families that they're better off without, I'm afraid that's just too depressing for me," he told her, keeping his voice deliberately low. He knew Maya couldn't hear him, but there was a part of him that thought somehow the vibrations from his tone would register with her.

January smiled. "Not like the happy-go-lucky life of a homicide detective, is that it?"

He nodded, knowing that what he'd said might come across a little hypocritical, but he did view what he did as a service to those whose lives had been affected by deadly crimes. "We each dance to the music we like," he told her.

Coming to a stop in the dairy aisle, January stared at the detective. "What does that even *mean*?" she asked him, stunned.

He gave her a mysterious smile. "You think on it and tell me when you've made up your mind," he said. "Meanwhile—" he put one hand lightly on Maya's shoulder to help guide her down another aisle "—let's see if we can finish up this shopping trip before nightfall." He looked down at Maya and gave her a wink.

The smile she returned said she understood him even if she didn't hear the words he'd said.

In the end, they loaded up on all the essentials, picking up bread and eggs, several packs of chicken breasts and legs, one package of hamburgers along with buns, and the required carton of milk for Maya, as well as a box of cereal with some sort of nutritional value.

For herself, January picked up an extra container of dark-roast coffee and a large container of creamer guaranteed to sweeten her coffee as well as rendering it a very pale color.

Sean looked down at the creamer. "I take it you don't like black coffee."

"Only as a last resort if there's nothing else," she confessed. "Otherwise, life's just too short to drink sludge."

"Is that what you think of black coffee?" Sean guessed.

"No," she answered with a straight face. "I also think it's good for fixing potholes and cracked tar."

"You know," he said, reevaluating the coffee he had had at her place when he dropped by that morning, "I thought the coffee tasted kind of funny when I had it this morning."

"And yet you drank it like a trouper." January pretended to marvel.

"Hey, I'm a Chicago police detective," he told her with a smile. "I've learned how to put up with a lot of things." And then Sean glanced at Maya, who looked as if she was trying to follow what was going on even though January wasn't signing anything at the moment. "Why don't you ask her if she wants any cookies or ice cream?"

That, she realized, had been an oversight on her part, not because she wanted the little girl to eat only healthy foods but because she herself rarely indulged in anything that, for the most part, came under the heading of junk food. While that was a healthier way to go, she knew the worth of sweets when it came to a child and she didn't want to impose her own standards on someone as young as Maya.

She signed Sean's question to the little girl and was

immediately on the receiving end of an enthusiastic response.

"You certainly called that one right," January congratulated the detective.

"Well, that really wasn't much of a challenge," Sean responded. "I never met a kid who didn't like cookies or ice cream. All things sweet, actually."

"Since we've already picked up all the basics—and then some," January said, looking into the cart, "let's see if we can find something to appeal to Maya's sweet tooth."

With that she guided the little girl and the cart to the cookie aisle.

After Maya debated for several minutes and finally made her choice—several kinds of cookies, including mint chocolate chip—the next stop was the ice cream aisle.

That choice turned out to be even more difficult. There were so many flavors to choose from. Maya finally narrowed it down to three.

Watching her try to decide between the different flavors, Sean finally turned toward January. "Why don't we just get all three? This way she has a variety to choose from—my treat," he added, in case the extra cost might be why the social worker would hesitate.

"I wasn't thinking about the price," she told Sean. "I was thinking about the temptation of having so many flavors so readily available," January admitted.

"Well, the princess doesn't strike me as the type to break into your refrigerator in the middle of the night and gorge herself on ice cream," Sean told her, smiling down at Maya.

"You're right," January confessed with a sigh. "I'm overthinking the situation—as usual." When he looked at her, curious at her admission, she explained, "In my line of work, I always try to be at least three jumps ahead."

"I can understand that, but why don't you just try being in the moment and enjoying that for a change?" he suggested.

Damn it but the man was good, she thought. It bothered her a little, because she was the one who was supposed to be that way, not him. Still, it didn't detract from the fact that he came across as a man who didn't just do things by the numbers.

She peered at him as they moved away from the ice cream aisle. "Are you sure you don't have any kids, Stafford?"

"No, but I've got cop instincts," he answered. "Let's go get this paid for." As he smiled at Maya, Sean took control of the cart.

January had the impression that the little girl would have gladly followed him to the ends of the earth and back if that was what she thought he wanted.

She caught herself thinking that she really didn't blame Maya one bit.

Chapter 11

Sean wound up staying for dinner.

After going out of his way as he had, January felt she at least owed him a meal. She had intentionally bought extra chicken cutlets so she could make Chicken Parmesan, a meal that came across fancier than it actually was.

She knew having Sean at the dinner table would make Maya happy, and if she were being totally honest, it didn't exactly make her feel as if she was enduring a hardship, having Sean at her town house.

Despite the fact that he didn't know how to sign, Sean got along well with Maya, managing to entertain her as January prepared dinner.

After the meal had been consumed, Maya, looking as if she couldn't contain herself any longer, signed a question to January.

Watching the little girl, Sean sensed that whatever she was asking might have something to do with his being there—especially since she pointed toward him.

"What's she saying?" he finally asked January.

The social worker chose to answer Maya before addressing Sean's query. Signing, she shook her head in response to Maya's question, then turned toward the detective.

"She wants to know if you're staying the night with us," she told him.

"No," Sean answered, looking at Maya. *Not that it isn't tempting*, he caught himself thinking. "That reminds me," he said to January. "I'd better get going. I've still got some paperwork to catch up on."

"Ah, yes, the glamorous part of police work," January commented, remembering the way one of the people she associated with said her husband referred to the dreaded paperwork that cases generated.

Rising from the living room sofa they had all adjourned to after dinner, January offered, "I'll walk you to the door, Detective. *We'll* walk you to the door," she amended when she realized that Maya was right behind her, ready to shadow her every move.

"An escort comprised of two lovely women. Who wouldn't welcome that?" Sean mused.

January signed what he had just said to Maya, who beamed at Sean, her eyes shining.

"You know," Sean said to January as he paused by the front door, fighting the urge to linger. "I could stay a little longer…"

As appealing as Sean seemed right at this very minute, she wasn't going to allow herself to get roped into saying yes. "A little longer" had a way of transforming into something greater and she couldn't allow herself to get distracted. Maya was her main, and *only*, focus.

"No," she told him. "Like you said, you have work to do and we've kept you here long enough. Besides, it's close to Maya's bedtime."

The news surprised the detective. "You've managed to establish when her bedtime is?" he asked.

"Not exactly," January was forced to admit. "I gave her the same bedtime I was made to observe when I was her age."

That brought him to another question. "You know her age?" he asked, glancing at Maya.

She was glad to give Sean at least one positive answer. "That I did establish," January confirmed. "I asked her if she knew how old she was this morning and she nodded vigorously, holding up five fingers." She smiled at the detective. "Maya's five."

"Well, that's good," he replied. "But nothing so far on her last name or her address, right?"

"Right," January signed. "I'm still coming up empty on that—for now."

Sean grinned. "So, now you're an optimist," he concluded.

She leaned into him, unaware that it caused him to catch a whiff of her light, floral perfume. "I'll let you in on a little secret. In this line of work, I have to be, or I'd wind up crying myself to sleep every night," she confided.

Straightening, she told herself it was time to have

him leave before she thought of an excuse to get him to stay permanently. "All right," she said, signaling an end to the evening. "You'll give me a call as soon as you know anything about her DNA?"

He thought of reminding her about the time he had already told her it was going to take, then decided it wouldn't do any good.

"You'll be my first call," Sean promised. "By the way, you make a really great Chicken Parmesan," he said by way of parting.

The compliment warmed her more than she would have expected. "Thanks. I'll look for your endorsement if I ever decide to open a restaurant." A whimsical smile played along her lips.

Her smile sorely tempted him, drawing him in and making Sean *really* want to kiss her. But he exercised restraint, knowing that to give in would be going way over any line he was allowed to cross. He was a police detective working a case that involved the little girl January had temporarily taken into her home, and that was where their connection began and ended. He couldn't afford to let himself lose sight of that.

No matter how much he wanted to.

"Don't forget to lock up," he reminded her as he started to go.

"Yes, Detective," she responded in a sing-song voice. "I also have an alarm system I plan to engage the minute I shut—and lock—the front door. Now go."

"Yes, ma'am." Sean saluted. And then he turned toward Maya, and to the surprise of both January and the little girl, Sean signed, "Goodbye."

Overjoyed, Maya signed the same thing back to him, her eyes dancing.

"I'm very impressed," January told the homicide detective.

"Don't be. I used the search engine on my computer," Sean told her.

"But you did think to use it, so I'm still impressed, Detective." She smiled her approval at him.

"Call me Sean," Sean prompted.

She inclined her head, humoring his request. "Good night, Sean."

"Good night, January," he said just before he walked to his vehicle, still parked in front of her house. He couldn't resist saying one last time, "Don't forget to lock up."

January sighed, murmuring something under her breath she was glad that Maya couldn't hear as she closed the front door. She shook her head. The man had to ruin it, she thought.

"C'mon," she signed to Maya. "It's time to get you ready for bed."

Maya seemed disappointed. "So soon?" she signed, crestfallen.

"It is not soon," January informed her firmly. "It's late."

Maya looked as if she actually wanted to put up a fight, but the next moment she nodded, giving in.

January smiled and kissed the top of the little girl's head.

"Atta girl," she signed, or something close to it.

After she had gotten Maya ready for bed, January went downstairs to finish cleaning up in the kitchen.

Maya followed her down, but January hadn't really expected anything else.

"You lie down on the sofa," she signed to Maya. "I'll be finished what I'm doing here soon."

January turned away, then heard an unfamiliar noise. She was about to sign that she wanted the little girl to settle down when she realized that the noise wasn't coming from anything Maya had done. It was coming from outside the front of the house.

Her attention piqued, January went to the window next to the front door and looked out. Scanning the street, she saw a black sedan parked in front of the town house next door.

The same one that she had seen pass by her own home several times yesterday evening. What was it doing parked in front of the Walkers' place?

Weren't they still on vacation?

She couldn't remember if the couple had returned recently or not.

You're doing it again, Jan, she upbraided herself. *You're overthinking things. The Walkers probably came back from their vacation this week and they have company now. People with normal lives do that kind of thing. They have people over. They have fun.*

She needed to stop borrowing trouble. With that, she looked around her kitchen. She had cleaned up everything and put things away. Now it was time for her to do the same thing with herself and Maya.

"Okay, sleepyhead," she said, addressing the dozing child stretched out on her sofa. "Time to get you to bed." Saying that, January scooped up the little girl and slowly carried her upstairs.

"At least someone is going to sleep well tonight," she said, placing Maya in the bed next door to her own bedroom.

January stood there for a moment, just looking at the little girl before she finally draped the blanket over Maya. She pressed her lips together ruefully. Instead of looking after other people's children, she could have had one of these of her own, she thought with a trace of longing.

"Right. Just what the world needs, another Immaculate Conception." She mocked herself because that would be the only way she would be able to have one of her own. She had no social life to speak of, other than the fund-raisers she attended from time to time with friends of her parents who were old enough to—well, be her parents. No chance for romance, much less a child there.

"You're doing just fine, Jan," she said aloud. "Stop feeling sorry for yourself. You live a great, fulfilling life. Now drop the pity party."

With that, she went into her bedroom. This time, unlike the previous night, she changed into an old set of pajamas she favored and then crawled into her bed.

The second she did, she realized that she could barely keep her eyes open. January was just about to drift off to sleep when a sudden noise penetrated her consciousness.

Her eyes flew open.

She knew that noise. It was the one made by her back-door alarm.

Someone was trying to come in.

January immediately thought of the black sedan she had seen earlier. The same one she had seen driving around yesterday.

Bolting out of bed, she paused only long enough to grab her cell phone—not even her shoes. Moving as fast as she could, she flew into Maya's bedroom.

"C'mon, baby, we've got to go," she signed as quickly as she could.

Maya had barely opened her eyes. January wasn't sure she had even gotten her message across to the girl, but there was no time to stop and sign it again.

They needed to hide.

Now.

There was a deep closet at the back of the second floor that had initially been put in as a panic room. The first owner had had it installed when he bought the town house. It was generally known that the senior citizen was a rich recluse who everyone had said was basically paranoid.

When she bought the town house, January had used the panic room as a storage area for things she meant to eventually go through and get rid of. The only problem was, she had never managed to find the time.

Her heart pounding as she held on to Maya, January hurried down the hall and made her way into the panic room now. She was praying that the lights inside still worked. She couldn't remember the last time she had tested them.

Completely awake now, Maya looked at her with sheer panic in her eyes.

It killed January to scare the little girl this way, but she had no choice. Someone was in her house and she couldn't think of any reason for them to be there other than that whoever had killed those three men in the warehouse had realized that there might have been a witness to what they had done. They had obviously tracked her down and were here to eliminate Maya before she could point them out.

This time, January didn't feel as if she was overthinking the situation. If she was, for some reason, then this was all Stafford's fault and he had to get himself over here to make sure that everything was all right.

Signing for Maya to sit down on the floor and give her a few minutes, January quickly tapped out Sean's number on her cell phone. She had programmed the number into her phone earlier that day.

Sean answered on the third ring.

Convinced that January wouldn't be calling him at this hour for some inane pillow talk, he picked up his cell and immediately asked, "January, what's wrong?"

"Someone's trying to break into the house," she answered in a breathless whisper. "I think he or they might already be here. Where's the damn police patrol you said was supposed to be out here, driving by my house?"

Her voice had gone up. If January was hiding, she sounded much too loud, Sean thought. That prompted him to ask, "Where are you right now?"

January took in a deep breath to try to steady her nerves.

"There's a panic room on the second floor of this house. Maya and I are in there right now, but I have no idea how secure it is. It came with the town house." Before he could ask, January told him, "I use it for storage."

She hadn't said anything about a panic room before, but that was a conversation for another time. "I'm leaving right now," he told her, dropping everything he'd been working on. "Hang tight," he instructed.

As he ran to get his vehicle, Sean put a call in to the detail he had assigned to maintain a patrol around January's town house.

"Hemmings," the patrolman answered.

"Hemmings, this is Detective Stafford. I'm on my way to the Colton town house. January Colton just called to tell me that someone is breaking in. You're supposed to be patrolling that area," he reminded the officer.

"Sorry, Detective. We're not there because Jonah and I got called away on another case," the police officer apologized.

"Another case?" Sean repeated in disbelief as he got into his vehicle. Securing his seat belt, he started up the car. "I had you doing *surveillance* on Ms. Colton's house," he told the officer sharply.

"Sorry, sir," Hemmings apologized again. "Lieutenant Walters said he needed us for something a lot more pressing than a babysitting detail. His words, sir, not mine. Again, I'm really sorry, Detective," the officer repeated.

Sean could feel his blood pressure going up. "Yeah, right."

Furious at being overridden without even the courtesy of being told, Sean terminated the call to the patrolman. The next moment, he was putting in a call to the dispatch desk.

"Nine-one-one, what is your emergency?" a calm female voice on the other end asked.

Sean identified himself, giving the dispatch desk his name and badge number. "There's a break-in taking place right now," he told the woman, then recited January's address. "The owner is home with a little girl. I think the people breaking in are involved in a drug gang and they believe the child was a witness to a triple homicide." He stressed every gory detail he could think of to get the police there as fast as possible.

For good measure, he ordered, "Get there now. I'm on my way and about ten minutes out. I had a patrol car cruising the area, but I'm told they got pulled for another assignment."

"I can check on that for you sir," the woman volunteered.

"Don't bother. Just get someone out there right now," he instructed, then repeated, "The little girl could have been a witness to a triple homicide and whoever is responsible could very well be trying to eliminate her, as well."

"I've got two patrol cars in the area," she informed him.

Sean never hesitated. "Send them both!" he ordered, stepping on the gas as he turned on his siren.

Chapter 12

The one thing that Sean had never managed to do, either as a policeman or as a homicide detective, was to effectively divorce himself from an ongoing situation. More specifically, he couldn't manage to separate himself from the details of any case he was investigating.

He envied those in the police department who could compartmentalize their minds or put up barricades within themselves so that what they saw or were dealing with did not weigh heavily on their minds.

Although Sean was able to maintain a calm outward facade, he just couldn't seem to do that inwardly, no matter how much he wanted to. Once he was on a case, he lived and breathed it until it was finally resolved, one way or another.

And then there were those cases that he couldn't

seem to put to rest because, even now, they hadn't been properly resolved.

Right now, he was vividly imagining someone—or several someones, for that matter—breaking into January's town house. Sean summarily cursed the patrol car that was supposed to have been in her vicinity—but wasn't.

If anything happens to January or Maya—

Sean abruptly blocked the thought from his mind, staunchly refusing to entertain it. He just couldn't allow himself to go there because to carry the thought out to its possible conclusion seemed much too horrible to contemplate.

Sean pushed down on the accelerator. The speedometer went to eighty—then past that.

With an eye out for traffic—and his throbbing heart lodged in his throat—he went faster. He just wanted to get there.

He'd estimated getting to her town house in ten minutes.

He got there in just under eight.

To his relief, the two patrol cars that dispatch had told him they were sending had already arrived.

Coming to a screeching halt in front of January's town house, Sean's vehicle had barely stopped running when he leaped out and went racing up the walk.

The front door was standing wide open. He couldn't make up his mind if that was a good sign or not, he only knew that his heart was pounding so hard against his chest, it felt as if it would crack through his rib cage at any moment.

One hand on the butt of his service revolver, the other holding up his identification for the benefit of the two officers he saw just within the foyer, Sean announced, "I'm Detective Stafford. Where are they?" Before either could answer, he shot a second, even more urgent question at them. "Were they hurt?"

Before either officer could speak, Sean had his answer. January was standing barefoot in her pajamas, holding a huddled Maya in her arms. January had apparently, just this moment, come down the stairs.

His first inclination was to throw his arms around both of them and hold them to him, but he managed to refrain. He had a feeling that January wouldn't appreciate this show of emotion right now.

"We're all right, Sean," January told him in a voice that indicated she was clearly shaken.

"We found them in what looked like a panic room, sir," the first officer, Jim Crawford, told Sean. "She had just opened the door. Although the lock on it looked kind of flimsy. I'd have it replaced, ma'am, if you want it to be of any real use."

Sean had a more important question for the officers. "What about the intruders?" he asked. "Did you get them?"

The other officer, Jacobs, an older man with thinning gray hair, spoke up. "We saw two men, dark clothes, medium build, running from the house. My guess is that the sirens must have scared them away."

Sean could only imagine what January must have gone through. He didn't want to think what could have happened if the intruders hadn't taken off but had managed to break into the panic room.

"Yeah, thankfully. Are you two all right?" he asked the social worker, stroking Maya's head in an effort to convey a sense of calm to the little girl.

January nodded. "Getting there," she answered honestly.

Sean had never been one to shirk a responsibility or to try to cover something up he thought might be his fault. And this, he felt, could very well have been his fault.

"I'm really sorry you had to go through this," he told January.

She was doing her best not to get angry, but that anger wasn't directed at him. She felt that there had to be some miscommunication at fault here.

"Where were the police officers you said were patrolling around here?" January asked.

Sean was having trouble controlling his outrage. "They were apparently called away on another case. No one told me."

"Well, if you didn't know, you didn't know," January said, resigned. She told herself that getting upset over what had happened wouldn't lead anywhere.

"That's no excuse," Sean bit out, furious about the oversight. "Luckily, Jacobs and his partner and a second squad car were in the area," he told her, but there was no abating the red-hot outrage he felt. "I'm sorry you had to go through that."

January didn't want the detective blaming himself. "Well, it's not your fault."

"Oh, but it is," Sean said, contradicting her assumption.

Her eyebrows drew together. "Maybe it's because of the hour," she told the detective. "But I don't understand." She looked up at him. "Why would it be your fault?"

"Because I'm thinking that whoever broke into your house had to be after Maya. That means that they followed me from the police station parking lot to your house. I am sincerely sorry, January, if I was responsible in any way for bringing those thugs to your doorstep."

She looked at him and saw the genuine regret in his eyes. He was sincerely sorry and there was absolutely nothing to be gained by making him feel even worse about it.

"Well, you didn't do it intentionally," she said, absolving him of the guilt. "But now what?" She glanced at Maya.

Maya had to be protected at all costs and they both knew that.

"I'm not leaving you unprotected again," Sean promised her.

That sounded good, but she wanted specifics. "What does that mean exactly?" she asked Sean, then made a guess. "Are you planning on camping out in the middle of my living room?"

"No, I'm taking you and Maya to my place," Sean informed her seriously, explaining, "You're moving in with me."

January hadn't expected that. "With you?" she repeated a little uncertainly. "Do you have enough room?"

"I have enough room," the detective assured her.

"Besides," he added with a smile, "Maya's little. She doesn't take up much space." There was a fond look in his eyes as he looked down at the little girl. And then he raised his eyes to January again. "Why don't you go and pack a few things for you and Maya? And then we'll get going. The sooner I have you out of here, the better."

This was really happening, January thought, stunned. It almost felt surreal. She needed to focus, to center her thoughts on things she could control. "How much should I pack?" she asked.

"Why don't you pack enough clothes for about five days," Sean told her, doing a quick estimate. "If you wind up staying at my place for longer than that, we can always come back here and get some more of your things."

January blew out a breath, frustrated. It was hard wrapping her head around this turn of events. "I feel like a nomad," she confessed as she began to go up the stairs again.

"Better a live nomad than the alternative," Sean quietly pointed out.

He was right, January thought, pressing her lips together.

She was doing her best not to lose it.

She was a Colton, damn it. And Coltons could handle anything that was thrown at them.

January started up the stairs again.

Maya looked torn between following January and staying with her protector.

Seeing her dilemma, Sean made a decision. "Wait up, January. You're going to have company." And with that, the detective took Maya's hand and went upstairs behind the woman.

Coming to the landing, January looked at the little girl. "Are you going to help me pack?" She smiled as she signed the question to Maya.

For the first time since this whole terrifying thing had started tonight, Maya smiled at January and nodded her head.

"Good," January signed back to her, saying the words aloud for Sean's benefit. "I could use your help."

"You know, I really appreciate that," Sean told January as he followed her and the little girl.

"Appreciate what?" January asked, not sure what the detective was referring to. Right now, the inside of her head felt like a giant jumble. It was hard thinking clearly and keeping everything straight.

"That when you sign to Maya, you say all the words out loud," Sean said.

"Oh, that. Actually, I do that as a form of reinforcement," she confessed. "I say something out loud because it seems to help my fingers make the right moves to convey the words."

"Well, whatever the reason," Sean said, "I fully appreciate not being kept in the dark about your communication. It's hard enough on me not to know what's going on."

"Think how Maya feels," January reminded the detective.

He flushed, embarrassed that he had made it seem that he was emphasizing himself. Maya was the important one in this.

"Yeah," he agreed. "You're absolutely right."

Packing, January caught herself smiling at the detective. In her experience, there weren't many men who would be willing to give a woman they hardly knew her due the way he did.

Detective Sean Stafford, she thought as she got another pair of jeans out of the closet, was a rare man indeed.

The next moment, she ordered herself not to get carried away. She knew that she had a bad tendency to do that when she dropped her guard—and this was definitely *not* the time for that.

Forcing herself to focus, January raised her guard again.

Moving quickly, she managed to pack one suitcase for herself in short order.

"What about Maya?" Sean asked. Watching January pack, he noticed that the only clothes that had gone into the suitcase were the ones that fit the social worker.

"Well, we had plans to go clothes shopping tomorrow," January told Sean. "But after what happened tonight, I suppose that's out now."

Sean looked at her. "Why?"

Was he playing games, or just testing her? "Well, because you just said we were going into hiding," she reminded him.

"No, what I said was I was transferring the two of you to my place. I didn't say anything about actually physically going into hiding," he told her.

Okay, this *was* a test, she decided. She wasn't about to have him trip her up. "I just assumed that going to what amounts to a 'safe house' wasn't going to include any shopping sprees on the agenda. Was I wrong?"

"No, not a shopping spree," he agreed. "But there isn't anything against going to buy some much needed clothing for a pint-sized princess," he told her, smiling at Maya.

Every time he found himself looking at Maya, Sean couldn't help smiling. By the same token, he couldn't help feeling furious and incensed that someone out there was willing to heartlessly do away with the child because she had had the misfortune of being in the wrong place at the wrong time.

Sean was beginning to think that she had nothing to do with the dead men who had been part of the drug organization.

For all he knew, Maya had just gotten lost while she was out with someone from her family. Without any identification on her and a limited ability to communicate, the little girl had been at the mercy of whoever's path she had wound up crossing.

Luckily, he thought, the path she had crossed had been his. Otherwise, who knew where she might have wound up? He abandoned the thought because to go on with it made him sick to his stomach.

"So, how about it?" he asked January. She had closed her suitcase so he picked it up and carried it down the stairs for her. Maya was right behind him. "You think you might be up for a small shopping excursion tomorrow, once you two get some beauty sleep?"

To be honest, she was having trouble thinking past the moment.

"Right now," January admitted, "sleep seems like a million miles away."

"Oh, it's a lot closer than that," Sean assured her. "And I've got a very comfortable mattress in my guest room."

"Guest room," she repeated, stressing the singular. "Not rooms?"

He shook his head. "Sorry, just the one," he told her. "After all, I'm just a poor public servant. What that means is that I can afford a two-bedroom apartment, not a fancy town house. It is on the second floor, though." In case January didn't follow him, what he was telling her was a good thing. "That means we can hear the bad guys coming."

She knew he was trying to make light of the situation in order to put her at ease and she did appreciate that. But the whole ordeal was still far too fresh in her mind for her to make peace with it yet.

January highly doubted that she would be able to sleep at all for the remainder of the night, much less get enough sleep to feel refreshed enough in the morning to be able to go on this excursion he was proposing.

Still, January reminded herself, she had been able to function on essentially an eyedropper's worth of sleep several times before. She could certainly do it one more time.

Standing on the first floor, she looked around for a moment. The first set of police officers had left, but the ones who had arrived in the second squad car were still there.

"Are you looking for something?" Sean asked January. "Maybe I can help."

"No, I'm just trying to see if I've forgotten anything essential I might need for my sleepover at your place," January answered.

Well, at least she was keeping a sense of humor about it, he thought. In his book, that made her a pretty remarkable woman.

Careful, Stafford. Keep it low-key. You don't want to get carried away, he warned himself.

"You know, if you think of anything you need later, like I said, we—or I—can always come back and get it for you," Sean told her.

"In other words, let's hit the road?" she asked, amused.

"Well, if you put it that way," he allowed. "Yes, in *any* words, let's hit the road." And then he turned toward the two police officers. "I want the two of you to follow me in your car. I am not taking any more chances with these two."

"Understood, Detective," said Officer Webber, the senior partner of the duo.

The officers were more than happy to be Stafford's escorts. They left the town house and January, glancing in Sean's direction, locked the front door and set the alarm system.

The officers traveled behind Sean's sedan, acting as his safeguard, until he reached his apartment with his precious cargo.

Chapter 13

"I know what you're thinking," Sean said as he let January and Maya into his apartment. He set down her suitcase in order to be able to reset his security system. "You're thinking that the apartment looks small."

January cut him short. He had come to their rescue and was now taking them in. There was absolutely nothing negative about that.

"Actually," she told the detective, "I prefer the word *cozy*." January smiled at him. "It seems to fit better."

Sean made eye contact with her. She was attempting to flatter him. There was no need for that. "Well I prefer the word *honesty*," he responded.

"Okay." She could go along with that. And, since he put such a premium on honesty, she had a question for him. An obvious one, in her opinion. "When was the last time you had this place cleaned?" she asked. While the dust wasn't exactly an inch thick, Sean's clothes were scattered around, looking as if they remained on the floor where he had dropped them—possibly in a hurry.

There was also the very real possibility that tidiness was not a really big deal on his list of priorities.

"Not sure," he deadpanned, then quipped, "My maid has the month off."

"Was that after she ran screaming from this place, or before?" she asked, humor playing on her lips.

He scanned the area through her eyes. "I guess I could stand to be a bit neater," he admitted.

January could only laugh in response. "You think?" she asked, amused, then added for emphasis, "You could stand to be a *hell* of a lot neater."

She glanced around the room again, imagining what the rest of the apartment looked like. "I take it that you don't do much entertaining," she commented.

He saw no point in denying it and attempting to maintain some sort of an image of a life. "My job doesn't exactly leave much time for that," he told her.

January would have definitely thought that a man as extremely attractive and sexy as the detective would have found some time to bring women into his life.

Actually, she mentally amended, she would have thought Sean would have had to beat those women off with a stick.

"I guess we have the same job." When he raised a quizzical eyebrow in response to her comment, she explained. "I don't have any free time, either. Being a social worker requires putting in a twenty-hour day—plus overtime," she added whimsically. Maya was yawning, drawing her attention back to the little girl. "Okay, show me to your guest room so I can put this munchkin to bed."

Sean looked at Maya. She was swaying where she stood.

"She looks like she's about to fall asleep standing up," he commented.

January laughed under her breath. "I'm counting on that," she admitted. Sympathy filled her eyes. "She really needs to get some rest."

"No argument here," Sean agreed. "This way." He paused only long enough to gather Maya up into his arms. She curled against him, resting her head on his shoulder.

January picked up her suitcase, following the detective.

"This layout is deceptive—actually larger than I'd expect," she observed, looking around as he led her to the second bedroom.

"Glad you approve. Tomorrow, after we buy some clothes for Maya, I'll see about getting the two of you set up in a hotel."

She didn't understand. January thought they had agreed about having Maya and her stay here. "Why would you do that?" she asked.

Sean set Maya down on the double bed.

Her lids fluttered. The little girl smiled up at him. It was obvious that she could hardly keep her eyes open.

The next moment, they were closed again. Sean hadn't even had time to tuck her in.

Thinking that January was undoubtedly better at it, Sean stepped back and left that up to the social worker to do.

"I thought you'd prefer that," he explained, referring to her question about the hotel room, lowering his voice before it hit him that he didn't need to. "You know," he continued in a normal voice, "a bigger bedroom with two double beds. I'd take the sofa," he added quickly in case January was worried that he was going to take one of the beds. Or that he wasn't going to be there.

"No," January said, vetoing the idea. "This arrangement is fine. Besides, this is your home territory. I think you'd be more comfortable defending it. It would certainly be more familiar to you."

"True," he said, thinking her comment over. It actually did make more sense to remain here. "Okay, if you have no objections, then, consider this your home until further notice. Can I get you anything?"

"Peace of mind would be nice," January answered wistfully.

His smile was sympathetic. "I'm working on it."

Not nearly fast enough for me, she thought. Out loud she said, "I know. Thanks. And no, I don't need you to get me anything."

"Good night, then," he said, reluctantly closing the door behind him, even though he would have really liked to have stayed with January in the room, at least a while longer.

January took in a deep breath and held it for a moment, then slowly released it. She spread her hand and pressed it against the door frame, imagining touching Sean's face.

"Good night," January whispered to the door.

After twenty minutes had passed, she knew she was far too tense and restless to fall asleep any time in the near future. Right now, she definitely needed something to make her relax.

But January had never been the type who believed in taking sleeping pills. Having any sort of alcoholic beverage to help her unwind wouldn't have been her choice, either. This was *not* the time to start doing either one.

That left hot tea, she thought. Hot tea used to do the trick when she was in college.

She thought the odds of Stafford having any tea in his cupboard were probably slim to none, but she supposed she'd never know unless she ventured out and looked around.

So, still in bare feet, January quietly padded into the kitchen. It was past two o'clock in the morning and the stillness that was both outside and in seemed to undulate around her, slipping under her skin.

She could actually hear herself breathing.

The apartment complex was silent. The residents in the area had long since gone to sleep.

For all intents and purposes, January thought, at this moment in time, she was alone in the world.

"Can I help you find something?"

The voice, coming behind her, made January jump and gasp in surprise as she swung her fist at him.

Standing behind her, Sean caught her arm before she could make a connection.

"Hey, Champ, I'm one of the good guys, remember?" the detective asked.

It took her more than a minute to still her pounding heart. Sean had definitely surprised her. She had thought that he was one of the home invaders, trying to break in again.

Realizing her mistake, it occurred to her that Sean was standing much too close to her. She could *feel* herself responding, growing warm. January struggled to regain control.

Finding her voice, she said, "I thought you were asleep." Damn, why wouldn't her heart stop pounding like this?

A faint smile curved his lips. "A good detective sleeps with one eye open."

"Is it always the same eye, or do you alternate?" She knew she was making inane conversation, but right now, she was stalling for time until she felt her brain was back in gear.

"That all depends on how long—or short—the night is," Sean said wryly. "What are you doing up?"

Belatedly, he released her arm before he gave in to the temptation to draw her closer and kiss that full mouth of hers. A mouth that, for some reason, seemed even more tempting here in his kitchen than it had been earlier.

Maybe the moonlight, pushing its way in through the blinds, had something to do with it.

But he sincerely doubted it.

"I couldn't sleep," she confessed to Sean.

"So I see," he replied. "I could offer you a drink."

But January shook her head, turning him down. "That would only make me more tense," she told him.

Sean nodded, understanding. "And if I gave you enough to make you relax, that would probably wipe you out for the next day," he guessed. He thought for a minute. "How about some tea?"

Even though she had come to search for some, she looked at him now in surprise. "You have tea?" she asked, adding, "You don't seem like the type, Detective."

"I'm not," he admitted. "Personally, I detest the stuff."

Okay, this was making no sense, she thought. "Then why—"

"Every once in a blue moon, my stomach acts up, and I found that drinking that swill helps settle it," he told her. "It tastes disgusting, but it does the job and that's all that really counts, right? Now, do you want me to make you some tea or not?"

January smiled and could feel her eyes crinkling. The man really was full of surprises.

"Yes, please," she told him. And then it occurred to her that she should be the one who was making the tea. There was no need for him to stay up. She didn't want to keep him from getting his rest. "Or you could tell me where you keep your pot and I can just boil some water. You don't have to stay up."

Sean pretended to study her face. "Are you telling me that you don't want my company?" he asked.

"No, it's not that," she assured him with feeling. "I'm just—"

He found it hard not to laugh, but he managed. "Then just sit down and shut up, Ms. Colton. I am not impressed—or intimidated—by who you are."

Sean was still kidding, but he also suspected that there were people who bowed and scraped before her because of her last name and who her family was. Personally, he found that to be dishonest. To his way of thinking, people should be treated for who they were, not who they were related to or associated with.

"I didn't say that you should be," she protested. She had no use for people like that. In her opinion, they were dishonest.

"Good, now sit," he told her again.

"I'm beginning to understand why those women I felt would be flocking to your door aren't flocking," she told him.

"You thought women would be flocking?" Sean asked, amused—and just a little mystified as to why she would even think that.

"Never mind, I'm delirious," she said, waving the remark away. "I don't know what I'm saying."

Sean looked at her, a wicked grin rising to his lips. But when he spoke, there was no trace of amusement in his voice.

"Understood."

Opening the cupboard, Sean looked on first one shelf, then the next, the contents of his cupboard pretty much of a mystery to him. He finally found a half-filled box of individually wrapped tea bags pushed to the back of a third shelf.

"I'm really not sure how old these are," he admitted. "If the tea winds up tasting ancient, feel free to toss it. I won't be insulted."

"If the tea bags are individually wrapped, they should be good indefinitely. Don't worry. I'm not picky," she assured him. "If it tastes reasonably like tea, that's good enough for me."

"We'll see." Sean poured the boiled water over a tea bag in a mug, then waited several minutes for it to turn into something acceptable. "I believe it's tea now," he told her, moving the mug in front of her. He left the tea bag in for good measure. "I've got a little bit of what passes for cream if you want to try adding that to the tea," he suggested.

She smiled. "No, I'll quit while I'm ahead. But thanks," she told him. "I do appreciate the effort."

He heard something in her voice and looked at her, all thoughts of continuing their banter gone. "Are you sure you're all right?" he asked, concerned.

"I am. Now. It's just that I can't get myself to stop thinking about *what if*," January confessed.

Sean shook his head. "You can't go there," he told her firmly. "Thinking that way will totally paralyze you and then you won't be any good to yourself—or that little girl you've taken under your wing."

January blew out a very shaky breath and took a long, slow sip of her tea. The warmth curled all through her, swirling in her chest then moving its way down through the rest of her.

"You're right," she told him.

Sean sat down opposite her at the table. "I usually am."

His unshakable confidence made her smile. "There's that ego again."

The detective didn't think of having an ego as a bad thing. "Hey, that ego is what keeps me alive," he told her.

January's green eyes met his. And then she slowly smiled. "Thank goodness for small favors," she said seriously.

"Or big ones," he corrected. "Now promise me that, other than being on your guard for Maya's sake, you are not going to spend any time dwelling on what *might* have happened. Just focus on the fact that the two of you managed to survive. By the way, answer a question for me."

"If I can," she equivocated, taking another sip of her tea.

"Just how did you happen to buy a place with a panic room in it?" he asked. "Did you actually want one?"

"That's just it," she told him. "I initially had no idea it was there. I honestly don't think that the Realtor who sold the town house to me even knew. In her defense, when you open the door, the first thing you think of is that it looks like a regular closet. It's not until you're actually *standing* in the closet and push against the back wall—which swings open—that you discover it's really intended to be a panic room."

Sean shook his head. "That must have been some surprise."

"Oh, it was," she agreed. "I accidentally found it

about a month after I moved in. When I did, I thought that someday, when I got married and had little people in my life, the so-called panic room would make a really neat place for them to play in and have creative adventures in." January looked into her mug. The contents were almost gone. "I never imagined that I would wind up using it for the very reason the guy who first installed it had in mind."

Sean heard the catch in her voice.

"You're thinking again," he admonished.

"Sorry." January flashed the police detective a quick smile. "Nasty habit I keep falling into. So," she said, clearing her mind and focusing on a new, lighter topic, "were you serious about that shopping trip you promised earlier?"

"Absolutely," he told her with all sincerity.

"But aren't you supposed to be working tomorrow?" she asked him. "How would you explain shopping for clothes for a five-year-old?"

"That's easy enough," he told her. "Guarding you and Maya is my new assignment. The warehouse where she was found was the site of a triple homicide. Maya was either an eyewitness, or the killer thinks she was. Sooner or later, he—or they—are going to come looking for her and try to find her. That's reason enough for me to be hanging around, guarding both of you." And then their eyes met. "Okay?"

January nodded, then drank the rest of her tea. Setting the mug down again, she told him, "You make a great cup of tea. Don't let anyone ever tell you otherwise."

Rising, she was about to take the mug over to the sink.

"I'll take care of that," Sean told her. "You just get to bed."

Starting to protest, January suddenly felt too tired to argue. "Okay," she agreed.

She was asleep within five minutes of entering the guest room and lying down.

Chapter 14

Sean's eyes flew open.

When he told January that he slept with one eye open, he hadn't been exaggerating. An unfamiliar noise had him instantly awake. It was coming from somewhere inside his apartment and he couldn't place it. It had to be too early for January to be up, especially considering how tired she had been.

Throwing off his blanket, Sean's feet hit the floor at the same time that he reached for his sidearm in the nightstand next to his bed.

He took the safety off as he silently made his way toward the front of the apartment and the source of the noise. His alarms hadn't been tripped, but the detective was well aware that a savvy intruder could figure out how to bypass any security system no matter what might have been used to arm it.

Moving as quietly as he could, Sean came into the living room, then froze in his tracks at the same time that he exhaled a long sigh of relief.

No intruder had broken in.

As near as he could ascertain, January was cleaning his apartment. Didn't the woman ever do what was expected of her? he wondered, irritated.

"What do you think you're doing?" he asked, putting the safety back on his sidearm.

January dropped the makeshift dust cloth in her hand, which, until an hour ago, had doubled as a kitchen hand towel. She pressed her palm against her pounding chest, trying to regulate her heart rate.

She turned around to face the detective. "You have *got* to stop sneaking up on me like that, Stafford, or I swear that you're going to wind up giving me a heart attack."

"That goes both ways, you know," Sean told her pointedly. He tucked his weapon into the back of his waistband. "Now, I repeat. What do you think you're doing and why aren't you in bed?"

"I got enough sleep," she replied simply. "As for your first question, I know you're not familiar with the idea, so you might not recognize it when you see it, but what I'm doing is cleaning."

His eyebrows drew together to form a dark, foreboding scowl.

"I know what you're doing," he informed her, annoyed. "But *why* are you doing it?"

"If you have to ask, you really don't understand the concept of doing it. Cleaning happens when a place *needs* it. And trust me," she said, her tone lightening, "your place really needed it."

Looking around now, she felt satisfied. She had made a dent in cleaning up the apartment, at least when it came to the kitchen and the living room. She told herself that she would tackle the rest later.

"You do *not* have to do this," Sean insisted. He assumed that the social worker felt she needed to pay him back for taking her and Maya in.

"Oh, but I do," she answered simply. Her reply surprised him. She wasn't doing it to pay him back, it was for an entirely different reason. "If the dust bunnies had gotten any worse than they were," she told him, "I would have risked losing Maya in them."

She said it with such a straight face, she almost sounded serious, Sean thought.

Just what he needed. A social worker who doubled as a comedian.

"Very funny," he commented.

"Sadly, not really," she told him. January looked around at her handiwork. "I'm going to stop now and look in on Maya. If she's up, I'm going to get started on making breakfast. This—" she gestured around the general area "—will be continued later."

"About breakfast," he interrupted. "I thought we'd just go to a drive-through place."

"No need," January told him cheerfully. "I looked in your refrigerator. You have eggs, you have bread, you have me. Everything you need for a balanced meal."

Maybe she was the type who needed to hear the words out loud, he thought. "Look, I did not bring you here to cook and clean."

"I know," she answered. "That's one of the perks of having me here. Had you *asked* me to clean, I might have dragged my feet a little. But you didn't ask, so I'm more than happy to do it."

Sean shook his head. That really didn't make any sense to him, but he had a feeling she wasn't trying for sense.

"You women are a very befuddling species," he told her in all seriousness.

January didn't bother correcting him. Instead, she just smiled as she headed out of the room. Her eyes looked like they were laughing at him. "Keeps you on your toes, doesn't it?"

That wasn't the only thing it did, he thought, watching January as she left the room, her hips swaying in an enticing rhythm that was beginning to reel him in.

The next moment, Sean sternly upbraided himself. Thoughts like that were bound to get him into trouble. It didn't take a crystal ball for him to know that.

Fully awake now, he went to the kitchen to get the coffee started. He found to his diminishing surprise that January had beaten him to it. There was a freshly brewed pot standing at the ready on his coffee maker.

In a pot that had been recently cleaned, he noted as he poured his first cup of the day. Just when did this woman get up? More important than that, how had she managed to do all this without waking him up until now?

Did she get *any* kind of sleep?

He doubted it as he looked around at what January had already managed to get done.

Somehow, she had cleaned the entire kitchen and had gotten most of the living room straightened up. Hell, he felt he was doing well if he managed to wash the dishes every couple of days or so—and that was without ever putting them away. His philosophy was that he planned to use the dishes at some point or other, so there was no real reason to empty the rack.

That rule of thumb had served him well so far.

"Guess who's awake," January said as she came back into the living room with Maya. The little girl was dressed, wearing the same converted blouse-into-dress that she had had on yesterday.

Sean noticed that her hair had been neatly brushed and rebraided. He also noted that not only did she seem less frightened than she had yesterday, but she actually looked happy.

"I don't need to guess," he said, lowering his voice before he remembered that Maya couldn't make out anything he said. But even so, he did add, "You're talking about my favorite princess." He enunciated the words right in front of her in hopes that, eventually, the little girl would be able to read his lips.

If for some reason Maya's stay here wound up being for a longer time, he would try to learn a few basics when it came to signing. Just a few frequently used words and phrases, because there was only so much that could be conveyed by a smile, he thought, trying not to get frustrated.

As she walked into the room, Maya surprised Sean by coming up to him and tugging on the edge of his shirt. It got him to bend down.

"Okay, I'm down to your level," he said, waiting to see what was next. "Now what?"

He sincerely doubted that the little girl could read his lips, but when he asked the question, Maya threw her arms around his neck and hugged him.

"I believe you have your answer," January told him. "And it looks like you won yourself a pint-sized heart," she added with a smile, smoothing down Maya's bangs. "Okay, now on to breakfast."

"I found the coffee," he told her, toasting her with his mug.

Her eyes crinkled as January smiled at him. "It wasn't hiding," she pointed out.

"I know that," he replied. "I'm trying to say thank you."

"Then say it. Nobody's stopping you. No preamble necessary." Her smile widened. "Was it to your liking?" she asked as she took out what she needed to make the simple breakfast. "The coffee," she prompted when he didn't respond.

"It wasn't as dark as I usually make it," Sean acknowledged. "But it was good."

"I wasn't sure how sludgy you liked it," she confessed. "So I took my best guess. Next time, I'll go a little heavier with the coffee—or lighter with the water." Then she decided that maybe it would be prudent to add, "If there *is* a next time."

"Are you resigning from the breakfast detail so

soon?" Sean asked, surprised she would give up so easily.

"No, I'm not planning on it," January told him.

She had lost him—again. "Then why the *if*?" Sean asked.

"I was making reference to the fact that you might get the bad guys," she told him. "Then there no longer will be a reason for Maya and me to play house at your place. The flip side of that is that you might find a member of her family and she will go with them."

"I'll say one thing for you. You certainly have more faith in the police department than most people do. Especially the people I've run into lately," he said, thinking of recent events that hadn't gone as well as he would have hoped.

"Sounds like someone might be badly in need of a vacation," she commented as she started preparing breakfast.

He laughed under his breath. The sound definitely lacked any humor. "No argument there, but that doesn't change my opinion about the way that a lot of private citizens in Chicago regard their local law enforcement agents."

She turned away from the stove for a second. "I'd say that, at the very least, you need to mingle with a different crowd of people—and soon." The moment the words were out of her mouth, an idea flashed through her mind. "And I have got the perfect solution for that," she declared happily.

He had to confess that the woman fascinated him.

She seemed very pleased with herself—and the look became her, not to mention that it drew him in.

"I'm almost afraid to ask," he told her. Despite the smile on her face, he found himself feeling more than a little leery about what she was going to propose.

"Don't be afraid to ask," she said playfully. "You're a police detective. Asking questions is a way of life for you."

January waited a beat as she cracked four eggs into a bowl.

When he didn't pick up the opening she had left for him, she felt she had no choice but to prod a little.

Turning to look at him over her shoulder, she urged, "So ask."

"Okay," he said gamely. "What is this perfect solution you have for me?"

"You, Detective Stafford, are going to come with me—with us," she corrected, looking at Maya, "to attend a family gathering."

"Any particular family you have in mind?" he asked, bracing himself as he watched her face and waited for her response. He had a feeling that he knew what she going to say.

"Yes, wise guy, a very specific family in mind," she told him, then said, "Mine."

"Since it's your family—and since I'm *not* family," he stressed, "wouldn't I be, you know, *crashing* this gathering?"

"Technically, you're my—*our*—bodyguard," she amended, glancing toward Maya. "That makes you as much a part of all this as my clothing. In case you're not following me, I wouldn't leave my clothing home, either."

Sean couldn't help but laugh. "That is a very novel way to describe it—but by the same token, very effective," he added, doing his best *not* to envision her without her clothing.

"As long as you get the message," January told him with a wide smile.

She put the eggs on low as she deposited the four slices of bread into the toaster. When they popped up, she buttered them all quickly, then placed two slices each on two plates and went on to distribute the eggs among the slices.

"So?" she asked as she set the plates down in front of Maya and Sean.

Sean flashed her a smile. He wasn't accustomed to being served in his own home. "Breakfast looks great," he told her.

"I know," she said, accepting the compliment as if there was nothing else he could have logically said. "But what about the invitation?"

"Shouldn't I wait to get it before I answer?" Sean pointed out.

It was clearly a stall tactic on his part and January knew that, but right now she really wasn't in the mood to play.

"You just did get it," she informed him. "From me."

"Well, if you put it that way," Sean allowed, "I guess the answer is yes."

"Finally," she declared as if she had just won a tournament that had taken way too long to win. "You certainly believe in making a person work for everything, don't you?"

"You mean that there's another way?" Sean asked innocently.

She didn't bother suppressing the smile that rose to her lips. "Yes, I believe they call it being straightforward."

"Oh, but this way, it just feels so much more rewarding when it finally comes through," Sean told the social worker.

She studied him for a long moment. "You know," January said, "with your rather unconventional sense of logic, you might be a Colton without knowing it."

Sean raised a puzzled eyebrow. "Is that your idea of a compliment?"

"No," she replied with an innocent expression, "just a simple fact."

Sean had been watching her. January had been moving around this entire time, preparing their breakfast and then serving it to them. There were only two plates, he noted.

"Aren't you going to eat?" he asked.

"Oh, I nibbled while I was preparing your breakfasts. And I did have toast earlier—two slices," she volunteered, knowing he would probably ask for a number.

"Nibbling?" he questioned. "Shouldn't you have more than just a nibble?"

She grinned at the detective, her eyes once again warming him.

Try as he might, he couldn't seem to get used to that. It was a pleasant surprise each time it happened. And he caught himself thinking about how it might feel, nibbling on her very tempting neck,

"A bodyguard *and* a nutritionist," she marveled, her eyes teasing him. "Anything else?"

"Yes," Sean answered seriously, doing his best to shut down these feelings threatening to run riot through him. "I also have a pretty short fuse when it comes to comments from wise guys."

"Duly noted," she said, nodding her head as she gave him the point.

"Just trying to look out for your best interests." Sean felt he needed to add that.

"And I appreciate it," she told him in all sincerity. "Now, I'll take care of the dishes, and then Maya and I will get ready for this shopping trip you're taking us on."

He took the plate out of her hand. "*I'll* do the dishes," he informed her. "You and the princess go get ready."

"Are you sure?" January asked, nodding at the dish. Most men weren't fans of washing dishes and he had already proven that he only did so when there was no way out. "It won't take me long."

"I'm sure," he said, still holding the dish in his hand. "Just because I don't wash dishes very often doesn't mean I don't know how. It just means I don't like to, which, the last time I checked, makes me a normal male. You find me a man who claims to like doing dishes and I'll show you a man who belongs in a museum under glass—or a notorious liar who's trying to impress the woman he's dating."

January grinned at him, amused. "As a matter of fact, you're probably right," she agreed.

Sean blinked several times and then pretended to cover his heart with both hands. Taking a "shaky" breath, he declared, "Be still my beating heart."

"You are also most definitely a wise guy," January told him.

"Guilty as charged." Then he ordered, "Now get going."

January took Maya's hand, turning toward the doorway. He didn't have to tell her twice.

Chapter 15

Sean had never been a fan of shopping for clothing. Ever since he became an adult, he had never entered a mall of his own volition unless it was an absolutely unavoidable necessity. The last time he remembered actually walking into a mall was more than two years ago. It had been to help Harry Cartwright, his former partner, go shopping for his wife's birthday. Harry had wanted to buy her something special, and true to form, he hadn't had a clue what to get.

Sean had gone with him during lunch for moral support. Three weeks later, Sean grimly remembered, Harry's wife and child were dead.

January saw the faraway, distracted expression on Sean's face as she brought Maya out to model one of her choices.

"Where are you?" January asked the detective.

Sean shook off the unwanted memory. "Nowhere where you would want to be."

January knew when not to pick at a scab and this had all the signs of being a bad one, so she tactfully backed off. But for Maya's sake, who was looking at him as if the sun rose and set around the man, she knew she had to get the detective to respond to the little girl.

"I think Maya's trying to impress you, Detective," January told him pointedly. "You need to smile your approval."

"Sorry," Sean said, his eyes washing over Maya as he warmly smiled at her.

Sean's smile, January noted, did wonders for both the detective and the little girl who was on the receiving end of that smile. Maya lit up right before Sean's eyes, causing the detective to respond even more.

January nodded her head. "Good," she declared with approval.

Sean wasn't sure if that was meant for him, but he saw no harm in taking it that way.

Taking his hand, Maya fairly skipped along beside Sean as they made their way through the store. He smiled at her, determined to make her feel safe and carefree despite the fact that he couldn't shake the feeling that they were being observed. It might have been his natural paranoia acting up, but he didn't think so. He remained vigilante and alert.

By the time the shopping trip was officially over—and they had managed to hit three different department stores during that time frame—Maya was completely outfitted with a supply of fresh new clothes. Sean had offered to pay for them, but January told him not to worry about it. Social Services would take care of it.

Sean knew for a fact that, the way that particular department operated, it would be a long time before January would be reimbursed. He had a feeling that she was actually footing the bill, but he wasn't about to press her on it. He trusted that if she was inclined to pay for Maya's wardrobe, January's family would probably take care of it in part.

"I think that Cinderella's going to be all decked out when it comes time to go to the ball," January told him once they finally returned to his vehicle.

Sean had carried almost all the items to the car while January and Maya each brought along a few items. And everything was summarily deposited into the trunk.

Putting away the last of it, Sean turned to see January sign something to the little girl. He assumed the message had something to do with what she had just said to him. He was sure of it when he saw the way that Maya laughed in response.

"My guess is that there's enough here for several balls," he told the social worker. "By the way, when is it?" he asked, because with everything that was going on, the date had slipped his mind.

It. Sean's question seemed to come out of the blue. She wanted to be sure they were on the same page before she answered him.

"Are you asking about my family's gathering?" she asked him.

"That's the only 'ball' that I know of," he told her, waiting for January to secure Maya in the car seat that had, in his mind, become hers.

"Saturday," she told him.

"This Saturday?" he asked uncertainly. It really didn't seem possible, since the event had almost come out of nowhere.

January was convinced that the detective was attempting to stall again, but why? Supposedly, in attending this event, he was just going to be her escort, the way he had for grocery shopping and now at the mall. Granted, attending the gathering wasn't going to be as impersonal as escorting them to the supermarket and the department stores at the mall had been. But it wasn't exactly as if she was bringing him as her date for the afternoon and definitely not as her "significant other," although the idea wasn't as off-putting as she might have once thought.

Sean was just going to be a warm body watching over Maya and over her, she reminded herself.

Why was he behaving as if he was suddenly spooked by the idea?

"Uh-huh," January confirmed with an attempt at nonchalance. "This Saturday." She glanced at him. "I didn't think you'd have a conflict since you said you were going to be our bodyguard until you or your department are able to find Maya's family as well as who killed those three victims in the warehouse. The same people," she pointed out, "who probably broke into my town house."

"No, I don't have a conflict," he replied, then decided

he might as well own up to the problem. "I just don't do well at family gatherings."

She looked at him. There was no *do well* about it, January thought. There was just being there, and he could certainly do that.

"Don't worry. Nobody's going to ask you to perform or do any magic tricks. You'll be fine. Tell you what," she said as she got into the front passenger seat and buckled up. "Why don't you pretend that you're undercover? That way, you can assume another personality during the time that we're over my parents' house. Would that make it easier for you?"

But he was stuck on another point. "Your parents' house," Sean echoed.

"Uh-huh. They're very nice people," she assured him. "Mom made Dad take down the photograph of the body of the last police detective he shot. It's no longer hanging over the fireplace," she told Sean with an incredibly straight face.

"Okay, point taken," Sean conceded.

"My parents are very nice people. My entire family is comprised of nice people. Don't get me wrong," she said, in case he thought she was just trying to whitewash her family. "There are times when they can make me crazy, but those times don't last and at bottom my whole family all mean well. Personally, without going out on a limb, I think that you'll find you like them.

"And, if you find any time during the course of the day that you just can't take it, all you have to do is say the code word and we'll leave," she promised.

"Code word?" Sean repeated. She hadn't said anything about a code word, he thought.

January looked over her shoulder to smile at Maya as they drove away from the mall.

"Uh-huh." He could swear that her eyes were laughing at him. "Everyone's gotta have a code word," she said solemnly.

"Okay," Sean replied gamely. "What's my code word?"

"Stratosphere," January answered. She smiled brightly.

He shot her a look. "Stratosphere?" he repeated incredulously. "How the hell am I supposed to work *that* into the conversation?"

January's smile just grew wider. Sean could have sworn that she lit up the interior of his vehicle.

"You're intelligent," she told him in all innocence. "I have great faith in you."

Sean snorted. *Yeah, right*, he thought. Out loud he said darkly, "Very funny."

"Not half as funny as the expression on your face," January said. "Relax, detective. I promise you'll have fun. Everyone in my family is easy to talk to—with the possible exception of my cousin Jones, but his only difficulty is with my uncle, not anyone else in the family. Personally, I think you and Jones will probably get along famously." She added, "He owns Lone Wolf Brewery, you know," to cinch the argument.

That managed to surprise Sean. "You're kidding," he cried, looking at her. "Your cousin actually owns that brewery?"

"I wouldn't kid you about that," she answered. "It's certainly an easy enough fact to look up."

Sean rolled that surprising piece of information around in his head, trying to absorb it. "Son of a gun," he murmured.

Satisfied that Maya was all right in her seat, January turned back around and returned her attention to the detective.

"Is there a reason behind that remark?" she asked, curious about his reaction to the information.

"Lone Wolf happens to be my favorite local brewery," Sean admitted.

That pleased her. It would certainly help matters when it came to the gathering. "See? You've already got something in common with a member of my family. This will be fun," she assured him again. "Really."

"Yeah, maybe it won't be so bad after all," Sean allowed, driving back to his apartment.

"Wow, you really know how to dish out high praise," January said with a laugh. The man would probably announce the advent of the second coming by saying, *Looks like He's back.*

Sean shrugged. "It's the best I can do at the moment," he told her. He tended to try to be low-key whenever possible. "Look, I said that I'm going with you. Why don't you just take the win and be done with it?"

"Okay. You're right. I'll take it," January said, then quietly added under her breath, "For now."

"You're bringing someone?" her mother asked later that evening when January called to tell her about Maya and Sean. She could hear Farrah Colton struggling not to sound as excited as she actually felt. "What's his name? Where did you meet him? Why haven't you—"

"Calm down, Mom," January said, raising her voice to be heard above her mother's. "Believe me, it's not what you think—"

"Not what I think?" her mother echoed. "Why? Is he a robot? A rubber doll? What? Talk to me, January."

January didn't know where to start. She didn't want to scare her mother, but she wasn't about to let her think that this was a boyfriend she was bringing. That would definitely kill any future between them.

"He's a police detective, Mom."

"So?" Her mother obviously didn't see a problem. "You know that I've always had the greatest respect for the law enforcement community. You're not handcuffed to him, are you?"

"No, I'm not handcuffed to him, Mom, but he is coming to this gathering in his police detective capacity," January told her.

She could tell that she had managed to lose her mother. The next thing Farrah Colton said confirmed her suspicions. "Okay, you're going to have to explain that to me, Jan."

Maybe if she went back to the beginning. "You know I didn't go on vacation with Simone and Tatum."

"I am aware of that," her mother told her. "Are you aware of the fact that they didn't go on vacation, either?" she asked, assuming that might have not registered with her youngest, even though she and her husband were throwing this party and wouldn't be having it if two of their daughters were unable to attend. Sometimes, her children got too involved in what they were doing and just became oblivious to key points.

"What?" January cried. Both of her sisters had told her that they were still going on that vacation. She felt a stab of guilt. Had they done this because of her?

"They decided to postpone until you were able to come with them. They didn't think it would be enough fun without you, which I think is a really nice compliment. They also said something about you taking in a little deaf girl because your department was short-handed and there was no one else available who could communicate with her."

Her mother paused, waiting for confirmation. When January didn't respond, she asked, "Did I get that right, January? Is that why you didn't go on that vacation?"

"Yes, Mom, you got it right," January told her. "Maya's been staying with me and it was necessary to get a protective detail for her. That's why Detective Stafford is coming with me. With us," she amended. "He's the protective detail." January was doing her best to word it so that she didn't wind up alarming her mother about how dangerous the situation potentially was.

She should have known that her mother wouldn't just leave the matter alone.

"Why does she need a protective detail?" her mother asked. "Is she in danger?" And then another question, far closer to home, occurred to January's mother. "Does that mean that *you* are in danger, too?"

"Mom, don't get ahead of yourself. I'm just taking

care of her until Sean...um... Detective Stafford locates her parents." She attempted to divert her mother by appealing to the woman's incredibly kind heart. "You can imagine how scared that little girl had to be, surrounded by a bunch of strangers in a world where she's unable to hear anything that's going on."

"That's why you were assigned to her."

January gave her mother a slightly more rounded explanation of the circumstances. "That's why I volunteered to take Maya in and be with her until she can be reunited with her family."

"How did she get separated from them?" her mother asked. "Can't you get her to tell you how that happened?"

"I'm working on it, Mom. First, I need to get her to really trust me," she told the woman. "That's why this gathering you're having will be so helpful. I'm thinking that maybe just having her around everyone, absorbing all those good vibrations, getting to feel secure—" January stopped abruptly, realizing that she wasn't being clear. "Oh, you know what I'm trying to say, Mom, right?"

She heard the smile in her mother's voice. "I know, darling, I know. You come with... Maya, is it?"

"Yes, Mom, it's Maya," January replied.

"Well, you know you're welcome to come with Maya and your police detective—"

January needed to nip this in the bud before her mother got carried away. This was all Sean needed to hear. "He's not *my* police detective, Mom."

"All right," Farrah said, changing her direction. "You

come with whoever's detective he is and we'll all show the three of you a very good time."

January wasn't completely convinced that there wouldn't be a problem. "You won't embarrass him— or me—will you?"

"Sweetheart, we wouldn't dream of it," her mother assured her. "Your happiness and well-being is our only concern and if, by extension, that includes Maya and Detective…?"

"Stafford, Mother. Detective Stafford," January told her. She knew she had already told her mother his name once and really doubted that the woman had forgotten it so quickly. Her mother was just enjoying this far too much.

"Detective Stafford," her mother repeated. "If that includes both of them, as well, well I say all the better. Now stop talking and start getting ready, dear."

"The gathering is tomorrow, remember, Mom?" January pointed out.

"Tomorrow will be here before you know it, darling," her mother said.

January sighed. "That's what you always used to tell me when I tried to put off doing my homework or studying until 'tomorrow.'"

"And I was right, wasn't I?" her mother asked, amused. "I also succeeded in getting you into the habit of studying before the very last minute. I'm very proud of that."

"Yes, I know," January answered with a laugh. "You're a great mother, Mom. Simone, Tatum and I are in complete agreement on that. Now, if you'll excuse me, I have to go. There're some things I need to do before we come over tomorrow."

"Just bring yourself, Maya and your *protective detail*, dear," Farrah added with emphasis. "That's all any of us want—or need—to see."

"And you will all be on your best behavior?" January asked one last time.

"When have we not been?" her mother asked innocently.

"You really want me to answer that?" January responded with a dry laugh.

Farrah chuckled, her tone vetoing that idea. "On second thought, you're probably tired. Get some rest, dear, and we'll talk tomorrow when you and your entourage get here."

She was about to tell her mother not to refer to Maya or Sean as being part of an entourage, then decided to drop the matter. Her mother, she knew, would be on her best behavior once she finally got to meet Maya and Sean. At this point January knew that it was a toss-up as to which one of them would hold the most appeal for her mother, although, in truth, she had to admit that she did have her suspicions about the matter.

Despite her concerns, January couldn't wait for the next day to come.

Chapter 16

"Hey, Sean, could you come here for a minute?" January called to him.

It was the day of the party and she was dressed and ready to leave for her parents' gathering. She had gone into the living room to make sure that Maya was still ready, as well, even though she had gotten the girl dressed earlier. January was taking no chances since she was accustomed to children who could get dirty and disheveled at the drop of a hat.

To her relief and delight, not only was Maya still neat and clean, she was actually entertaining herself. Sitting on the floor in front of the coffee table, the little girl was drawing on the sheet of paper January had given her.

Expecting to see wide, unrecognizable circles and squiggles, January was surprised at how well Maya was able to actually draw. The end result was a picture of animals gathered together. It was definitely better than most five-years-olds were capable of doing.

The girl had real talent, January thought.

Reacting to her summons and expecting the worst—because that was the nature of his work—Sean came hurrying into the living room. He hadn't tucked his shirt in yet, but his service weapon was in his hand and ready to use if necessary.

Seeing his gun, January realized how she must have sounded to him and she immediately apologized. "I'm sorry, I didn't mean to make you think that something was wrong." She gestured toward the coffee table at the drawing Maya was working on. "Look at what Maya drew while waiting for us."

Sean looked at the drawing more closely. To his surprise, he was able to make the figures out. "Is that supposed to be us?" he asked.

"Well, two tall figures and one short one with long brown braids. Judging from the clothing the taller figures are wearing, they're definitely supposed to be a man and a woman. So, taking that into consideration," January told him with a smile, "my guess would be yes, Maya made a drawing of us."

She slanted a glance at the detective. He wasn't picking up on the important part. "Look at it. She drew us as a family." She indicated the figures. "Look, we're all holding hands."

"Son of a gun, you're right," he said, smiling at the drawing. Maya looked up at him and he signed "Good," pleasing the little girl while surprising January.

"You just told her *good*," January said, amazed. He hadn't said anything about continuing to learn how to sign.

"I know," Sean replied as if being able to do so was nothing out of the ordinary.

January smiled at him. The man just kept surprising her. "You've been studying."

Sean merely shrugged. "I thought it might be a good idea to try to keep up a little," he said, as if learning to do so was no big deal on his part, even though January knew it had to be. The detective was incredibly busy. Learning how to sign, even in a very minor way, would have taken a lot of concentrated effort on his part.

The man really cared.

He looked back at the drawing. It was impressive for what it was. "She's pretty talented for a half-pint," he told January.

"And, on that note, I think we should be leaving," she said. "We don't want to be late."

"Why? Do the doors slam shut at the mansion if you don't arrive on time?" the detective asked. But it wasn't a hostile remark. His mouth curved as he asked the question.

"No, it's just not polite to be late, that's all," she informed him matter-of-factly. She had been raised to always be punctual. "And it's not a mansion. It's a regular house—just a little larger than most," she added, then felt she needed to tell him one more fact—or maybe two. "My parents' house and my uncle and aunt's house were built on the same property next to one another. The houses are exquisitely furnished. That's because both my mother and my aunt Fallon are interior designers. They have their own company."

"And your father and uncle are into developing medical technology," Sean recalled as he held the front door opened for January and Maya.

"You *have* done your homework," January said, impressed. "By the way, anywhere in that homework you did, did it happen to mention that my dad and my uncle Ernest are twins?"

"I might have read that somewhere," he replied vaguely, resetting the alarm system before he walked out to join Maya and January.

"Uh-huh. Did you also happen to read that my mom and my aunt Fallon were twins, too?" January asked.

That caused Sean to stop short for a moment before he finally got to his car and unlocked the doors. He held the rear door open so that January was able to secure Maya in her car seat.

The part about her mother and aunt had eluded him. "Twins marrying twins?" he asked, saying the words out loud as if to make sure that was what January was telling him.

She couldn't help laughing at the expression on Sean's face. He appeared stunned. She could relate to that.

"When you're a little kid," she told him, remembering various incidents from that time, "you think you're always seeing double. And then you start to think that everyone's parents have look-alikes. Wrapping your head around the fact that your parents are actually unique turns out to be a little harder."

"I'll bet. Well, if nothing else," he said as January got into the car on the passenger side, "today should really prove to be interesting."

"And fun," she reminded him, buckling up. "Don't forget fun."

"So you said," he told her as he started the car. At the time, he'd just thought she was trying to talk him into going, but now, he was beginning to think that maybe she was actually right.

As he started up the ignition, January realized that she hadn't given him her parents' address. "Oh, let me give you the directions," she offered.

But before she could say anything further, Sean told her, "Not necessary. I've already got them."

January could only shake her head in total wonder. "You really are prepared, aren't you?" she marveled.

He didn't see why that should surprise her. "In my line of work, my life could depend on that," he reminded her.

"Well, for today your life is secure. All you need to be prepared for is to enjoy yourself," she informed him. "If you ask me, I think you both could use it."

"I can see Maya needing it," Sean admitted. "But not me."

He could feel January looking at him. "Oh, I think you need it a lot more than you think, Sean," she told him. "If you ask me, you're in a dark place, Detective. You need to find a way to get out of there before it winds up swallowing you whole." Her eyes met his. He was blocking her, she thought. "I know what I'm talking about."

"Is that the social worker talking now?" Sean asked.

His tone told her that he was humoring her, but it also told her that she was right.

Sean was harboring something, something he didn't want to talk about. Maybe he had suffered some sort of breakup, January guessed. Or maybe it was something else, but whatever it was, it had definitely left its mark on the man and wounded him.

He looked as if he was visibly shutting himself off from her.

"I also volunteer for several charities and deal with a lot of emotionally wounded people," she told him, trying to explain why she felt he was being secretive about something.

"I see. Well, you save all that insightfulness for them," he told her. "With me, what you see is what you get. No trapdoors, no secret hiding places."

Smiling at him, January said, "If you say so, Sean."

"I do," he told her emphatically, his tone a little more serious than he had intended. Gripping the wheel, he stared straight ahead as he pressed down on the gas pedal.

"Um, Sean?" January tried to get his attention as he continued driving.

"Yeah?" he bit off, then instantly regretted it, trying to get hold of the temper that had gotten away from him.

"We're here," she told him. "Or, we were, except that you just passed it." She nodded toward the house that was growing smaller in the rearview mirror.

Sean bit off a sharp curse, aimed at himself. He was relieved that the little girl sitting behind him wasn't able to pick up on what he had just said. He needed to get a better grip on things, especially when it came to himself, Sean thought.

Frowning, he shot January a look. "You distracted me."

She caught herself grinning. "I think that's the nicest thing you've said to me so far," January told him. She tried to hide the grin.

Sean spared January a glance, seeing the fight she was waging. Several things popped into his head as a response, but what ultimately wound up coming out was, "The day's still young."

Why what was, for all intents and purposes, a throwaway comment would wind up warming her heart was anyone's guess, January thought. This was not the time to analyze it.

"Ah, something to look forward to," January said flippantly. "But let's just table that for now, shall we? Looks like we're here."

Turning in her seat, she signed as much to Maya, then got out of the vehicle.

Sean was already out on his side. "You think it's all right if I park here?" he asked. There was a lot of open space in front of the palatial house, but he wasn't sure just what protocol dictated and he didn't want to accidentally cross anyone.

"I'm sure that my mother would tell you that you can park anywhere you want to, short of in the birdbath," she told the detective with a laugh.

Then, because she was afraid that might somehow wind up intimidating him, she explained. "Because you rescued Maya and me from those intruders, you pretty much walk on water as far as she's concerned," she told him.

He nodded. "Yeah, well, since that's pretty much my job, I have no idea why that puts your family in my debt."

She flashed a smile at him. "We're a very close family and we're partial to keeping all the members alive," she quipped. Then, looking at the somewhat imposing house, a house she had thought of as home all of her life, she asked, "Ready?"

"Maybe you should give me another minute or so," Sean said. He knew that this should be like any other encounter, but for some reason, he felt as if he actually needed to create a good impression.

January had a feeling that in another minute, the detective would find a reason to either bolt or, most likely, remain outside, acting more like a protective detail and less like a guest.

She didn't want to drag him inside, but she also didn't want to have to explain to her mother why the man she was obviously looking forward to meeting had suddenly decided to disappear.

So, instead of giving Sean that minute he had asked for, January got out of the vehicle, took Maya by the hand and walked up to the front door. She heard Sean closing the car door behind her. She hoped that was a positive sign.

January rang the doorbell.

The next instant, the massive front door flew open, and as she had prophesied, Sean found himself seeing double. Both her mother and her aunt Fallon were standing in the doorway.

"Welcome!" her mother cried, delighted as she extended the greeting.

Equally pleased, Fallon's eyes swept over the police detective who had escorted her niece. She proclaimed, "You're here!"

Both women welcomed Sean with open arms at the very same time that they embraced the little girl they had been told about.

For her part, Maya seemed both overwhelmed and slightly enchanted at the same moment. Her head moved back and forth as she looked from one woman to the other, and finally to January, an obvious question in her eyes.

January quickly signed to Maya, introducing her to her mother, Farrah, and then to her aunt Fallon. Belatedly, she realized that she had neglected to do the same for Sean.

"Wow, where are my manners?" January admonished herself. "I'm sorry." The apology was meant for all three adults. "Mother, Aunt Fallon, this is Detective Sean Stafford. Our bodyguard."

"And here I was, feeling sorry for you for having to give up your vacation," said a tall, very pretty blonde, walking up to them. She momentarily gave Sean her undivided attention. "Hi, I'm January's cousin, Carly Colton." She put out her hand.

Sean shook it. It was obvious that he was trying to place her—and failing.

"I'm sorry, I don't mean to stare. It's just that you look very familiar," he explained.

"There might be a reason for that," Carly told him. "I'm a pediatric nurse at Chicago University Hospital. If you've ever had any reason to come by the hospital on police business or for any other reason, our paths might have crossed."

Her words unexpectedly brought back an image that he had struggled for two years to bury. It was never that far from his mind, but the mention of the hospital managed to quickly unearth it.

His expression grew grim. Carly didn't notice, but January did.

Unable to ignore it, January leaned into Sean and whispered, "Is everything all right?"

"Yes. Sure." Sean was quick to rally. "Just a little overwhelmed by how much your mother and aunt look alike."

He was lying, January thought, but for now she knew she had to let it go. Sean clearly needed space, and maybe even some time to cope with whatever was going on in his head.

So she said, "Well, if you think that's something, then you had better brace yourself."

He didn't understand. "For what?"

There was no need for her to answer because at that moment, a deep, baritone asked, "Was that the lilting voice of my youngest daughter, or am I just imagining things?" Alfred Colton, a tall, imposing man with very thick, dark-blond hair, walked into the front room.

January turned around, beaming at the larger-than-life man.

"You're not imagining things, Dad. It's me," January answered, affectionately kissing her father's cheek.

"So, you're not a figment of our joint imaginations," Uncle Ernest said, coming up to her other side and pressing a kiss to her cheek in turn.

"Wow." The word escaped Sean's lips without his meaning it to. He heard it belatedly and flushed as both men and January turned in his direction.

January was the first to say anything. "I told you they looked eerily alike."

That they certainly did, Sean thought, stunned despite having been warned ahead of time.

"January, that's no way to talk about your father," her uncle said.

Ernest's comment was echoed by his brother. "Or your uncle," Alfred Colton told his youngest daughter.

"In my defense, I don't think that Sean was prepared for just how very alike the four of you look," January said.

"Well, your mother and I don't look alike," her father teased.

"You know what I mean, Dad," January told him, looking at the foursome who had been the reason for so much confusion in her younger days.

"Uh-huh." Disregarding his daughter's words, Alfred Colton took Sean's hand and shook it. "Nice to meet you," he told the detective. "You're the first breathing male January ever brought home who wasn't in foster care."

January's face turned bright red as she cried in protest, "Dad!"

"Alfred." Her mother chided her husband at the same time.

Alfred Colton appeared the soul of innocence as he asked, "What did I say? It is true."

"Women," Ernest Colton said with a shake of his head. "Who can understand them? Am I right?" he asked Sean with a conspiratorial smile.

Sean glanced over at January. "Absolutely," he agreed.

The funny thing was, he found himself falling—not only for January, but for her family, as well.

At least, the members he had met so far.

Chapter 17

No one was as surprised as Sean at how much he really liked and got along with January's family. Not just one or two of the members, or because he felt he had to be polite to the Coltons who were, after all, a very big, important family in the area. Sean had never kowtowed to someone because of who they were or how much money they had.

But in this case, he quickly discovered that these people—every single one of them—were all genuinely nice and down to earth. He felt he could see through an act and these people really did seem like they took an interest in him as a person.

Sean found himself caught up in the various family dynamics playing out before him. Moreover, at no time did he feel as if any of January's relatives felt themselves to be above him in any manner, shape or form.

The detective was also surprised to find that he wasn't the only nonfamily member attending the gathering. Shortly after he, January and Maya arrived, he saw Cruz Medina in the group. Medina was Tatum Colton's newest employee at her restaurant. Since Sean had assumed that this was a family-only gathering, and that he and Maya were the exceptions, seeing another nonfamily member there was a surprise.

When he questioned January about it, she told him that her restaurateur sister had just hired Cruz as a sous chef for True and had brought the man to meet her family. It was her way of getting him entrenched. Sean found all of this to be unusual, given that he recognized Cruz from the Narcotics Division. As far as he was aware of, Cruz knew his way around a coffee maker, and that was the sum total of his culinary abilities.

Sean made no comment when they were introduced, but as soon as he found an opportunity to do so, he made his way over to Cruz.

Pouring a glass of wine for himself and one for the Narcotics detective, Sean handed the other man a glass and asked, "Hey, what's the deal, man?"

When Cruz raised his dark, expressive eyes to Sean's face, indicating his ignorance about the comment he had just made, Sean asked plainly, "Are you moonlighting these days?"

Since news traveled fast at the police station and rumors even faster, Cruz saw no reason to pretend. Sean, he reasoned, knew enough to keep this quiet.

"Something like that," Cruz replied evasively. Then he said, "Way too complicated to get into right now."

Just in case this was something other than he thought, Sean felt a warning of sorts was in order. "These are good people," he said to the man he knew as Harry Cartwright's new partner. "I wouldn't want to see any of them get hurt." The smile on Sean's lips never wavered, but there was no mistaking his warning. He was telling Cruz to be on his best behavior.

"Don't worry," Cruz said as he raised his glass to his lips. "I have no intentions of hurting anyone here. I have a completely different target in my sights, but that's all I can say on the subject right now."

Sean nodded his head, dropping the topic for the moment. "Understood."

"Hey, what are you two talking about?" January asked as she came up to join the two men.

"Just sharing some common interests," Sean replied vaguely. "Speaking of common interests—" he quickly scanned the room "—where's ours?"

He had really expected to find Maya hermetically sealed to January's side since the little girl wasn't with him at the moment. That she was with neither one of them worried him more than he let on.

"She's with Carly," January explained, pointing her out to the detective. She had kept one eye on the little girl at all times, even when she wasn't with Maya. "Everyone's doting on Maya," she told him with a touch of affectionate pride. "But, as it turns out, Carly also knows how to sign, and she and Maya have been talking up a storm, so to speak."

January looked again toward where she had left the little girl. Observing Maya with Carly and her mother now, she thought Maya was positively glowing. With a sigh, January said, "I think we're going to have a tough time getting her to come home with us."

The moment the words were out of her mouth, she immediately looked at Sean to see if he had caught her slip.

The look on his face told her that he had.

I'm going to have to be careful, January told herself. She hadn't meant to make it sound as if the three of them were a unit.

To her surprise, as well as relief, her inadvertent comment didn't seem to bother Sean.

It was getting harder and harder for her to maintain that barrier she had put up between them. Harder for her to remember that Sean was just here with her—and Maya—in a professional capacity. She found that his constant presence was generating some very *un*professional thoughts in her head.

And those thoughts were really beginning to get in her way.

"I agree," Sean was saying, watching the little girl. "Good thing that Maya seems to have such a soft spot in her heart for you."

"For both of us," January corrected emphatically. She wanted to give credit where it was due and to make Sean realize that, without even meaning to, he had formed a bond with Maya. But this situation couldn't go on indefinitely and she knew it. "Has any progress been made with that DNA match?"

"No, not yet," he told her. When he caught the sharp look that crossed her face, he quickly added, "but it turns out that the lab is really swamped, so it's going to take longer than the promised forty-eight hours to get back to us."

"It's getting really hard to be patient," she told Sean.

He caught the edge in her voice. His eyes met hers.

"Yes, I know," he replied, even though he wasn't thinking about getting the DNA results or anything even remotely close to that. Instead, he was thinking about the impatience that longing had created within him.

Apparently feeling as if he was intruding, Tatum's pseudo-chef took this opportunity to break away. "I'll see you around, Stafford," Cruz said.

Nodding at January, he made his way back to where he had left her sister.

"You two know each other?" January asked, mildly interested.

Sean had no desire to be caught in a lie, but at the same time, he didn't feel he should volunteer too much at this point.

"Yeah," he answered, leaving it at that.

January drew in a breath. At times Detective Sean Stafford could be the most uncommunicative man, she thought in frustration.

"From where?" she asked.

"Long story," he answered flatly.

She supposed that was meant as her cue to back off. "Maybe some other time," January replied.

She wondered if the man realized just how much slack she kept cutting him.

"Maybe," he agreed, leaving it at that. "Let's get back to Maya before someone in your family decides to permanently whisk her away." Sean began to make his way back to the circle of people around the little girl.

Despite the fact that a perpetual wall of silence surrounded her, effectively separating her from everyone else there, Maya seemed to be very happy, even thriving, in the ongoing atmosphere.

January began to appreciate the fact that, in every way except for one, Maya was a normal, happy little girl. It made the social worker in her more determined than ever to attempt to find the little girl's family and unite her with them.

January made a solemn promise to herself that, with or without Sean's help, she was going to make this happen for Maya.

They wound up staying at her parents' house a lot longer than January had intended. Initially, she'd thought that they would leave the gathering a great deal sooner than they did. She didn't want to abuse Sean's good nature.

But as it turned out, he was the one who demurred when she suggested leaving.

He seemed to be really enjoying himself, January thought. She had the distinct impression that the detective was not accustomed to this sort of celebration. Her guess was that, being exposed to it now, Sean was trying to absorb as much of it as possible.

January had watched in fascination as her father and her uncle took Sean aside at different points in the af-

ternoon and evening, undoubtedly sharing some sort
of guy thing that ultimately pleased and/or amused the
detective. She saw him smiling, *really* smiling.

For her part, she would have loved to be able to hear
what was being said, but she instinctively knew it had
to be something to do with "man talk," a term both her
father and her uncle favored. Quite simply, it referred to
imparting "wisdom" along the lines of older man passing down acquired knowledge to younger man.

She'd been afraid that Sean would initially brush
it off, but she discovered that she was worrying needlessly. Going by Sean's expression, he seemed to take
it all well, and each time she saw that his demeanor remained easygoing. Possibly, in part, thanks to his police training.

By the time they finally did leave the family gathering, Maya appeared to be all but spent. She did attempt, for a while, to get across how excited she felt.
For a little bit, her small hands seemed to fly, talking
almost nonstop, sharing as much as she could with January and Carly.

But then, perforce, Maya's hands grew still, and her
eyelids kept drooping, signaling she was about to lose
the battle against encroaching sleep.

By the time they finally reached Sean's apartment,
Maya had fallen sound asleep. She didn't even wake up
when January unbuckled her from her car seat.

Nor did she wake as Sean slowly picked her up from
that seat and drew her into his arms.

Careful not to jostle his precious cargo, the police

detective moved almost in slow motion. He didn't want to wake Maya up.

"I think she's completely worn out," Sean whispered, holding the small body to him as he began to go up to his door on the second floor.

"Sean, you don't have to whisper," January reminded the detective, once again pointing out, "Maya can't hear you."

"Logically, I know that," Sean replied. "But on some level, I think maybe she can. I know it's dumb."

"No, it's not dumb," January argued. "It's sweet. I know that's not something I'm supposed to say to a homicide detective, but it doesn't change the fact that I think it is. So sue me." She raised her chin as if she was issuing a challenge.

His mouth curved. "Suing is just about the *last* thing on the list of things I want to do with you," Sean confided as he came to the landing. Crossing to his door, he realized that he would have to shift Maya in order to get his house key out.

Which probably meant waking her up.

He looked over toward January. Positioning his hip in such a way that she would be able to get into his side pocket, Sean said, "Would you mind?"

January wasn't following him. "Mind what?"

He supposed he hadn't exactly been clear. "I can't get my key out to open the door without shifting and jostling Maya. But you can."

That didn't jibe with what he had told her earlier. "I thought you set the alarm before we left for my parents' house."

"I did. But I need to put the key into the lock to disarm the alarm so I can input the right combination in order to open up the door." He looked at her to see if she was following what he'd just said.

January rolled her eyes. "Oh, for the days when you could just kick down a door," she said with a wistful note in her voice.

"Yeah, right." He laughed, trying to envision her actually kicking down a door. "You and what army?" Shifting, he waited for January to slip her hand into his pocket in order to secure his house key.

January took in a deep breath and then slipped her hand into his pocket to retrieve the key. "I'll have you know I can kick down doors," she informed him. When he gave her a skeptical look, she qualified her remark. "Little doors in dollhouses, but still doors."

Sean nodded. "If I'm ever trapped in a dollhouse, you'll be the first one I send for," he told her with an aura of solemnity in his voice.

"Deal," January agreed.

Her hand seemed to tingle where she had slipped it into the pocket of his jeans. It had taken her longer to locate the key only because she was trying her best not to turn the hunt for the key into something a great deal more tantalizing and physical.

She failed.

It was exactly that.

But that was because she was trying so very hard to divorce herself from the process.

Finally securing the elusive key, she held it up in front of his face. "I got it," she declared. "Now what?"

"Use it?" he suggested. "Before the night gets too old?"

"Right," she murmured, utterly embarrassed that, just for a moment, she had managed to get *really* distracted by her hunting errand.

Slipping the key into the lock, she input the combination, then turned the doorknob and opened the door to his apartment. She quickly looked around the immediate area. "Nothing looks as if it's been touched."

"That's good to hear," he said, looking around himself. "But I am the detective, so I'd better act like one. I'll check everything out. You take Maya."

Very carefully, Sean passed the little girl to her.

"This must be what the changing of the guard feels like," January quipped, taking Maya into her arms. The little girl didn't even stir, she noticed with pride. "I'd better get her to bed," she told Sean.

"Not until I clear the apartment," he said emphatically.

She thought he was being needlessly overcautious, but she didn't want to spoil the night by arguing with him. *Better safe than sorry*, she reminded herself for the umpteenth time.

"You're right," she agreed. "I'll wait here with Maya."

She stood there, holding Maya against her, thinking that this had to be what having a child was like.

A warm, protective feeling flooded through her as she waited for Sean to return.

Someday, she promised herself. *Someday*.

She felt as if she had been standing there, waiting

forever, when Sean finally returned to the front of the apartment.

"It's all clear," he told her. "Nobody is in here except for us." He gently took Maya back into his arms. "I'll take her to her room and put her to bed. You look as if you're about to fall over if you try to do that."

"I'll have you know that I'm fresh as a daisy," she informed him.

"Right, a daisy that's been growing in the desert for the last two months—without any water." He laughed.

"Flattery is definitely not your strong suit," she said as she followed Sean to the guest bedroom.

"Maybe not, but observation is," he pointed out. "It's what I do for a living, remember?"

"I keep forgetting," she said, deadpan. "I guess that's why I have you to remind me." She watched as he laid Maya down.

"You want to get her ready for bed?" he asked, although if it were up to him, he would opt to leave the little girl dressed.

"I don't want to risk waking her up," she said, agreeing with him without realizing it. "This will do fine for tonight." And with that, she stepped back and accidentally bumped up against Sean.

Chapter 18

Without meaning to, Sean brushed his chest against her back. It was just the most innocent of contacts, and yet the moment it happened, January was on the receiving end of an electrical shock that went shooting right through her.

Sean reacted instantly without even thinking about it. He put his hands on her shoulders and slowly turned January around. There was nothing more to his action than wanting to steady her.

At least, that was what Sean told himself.

But when he turned January around so that she was facing him, he was suddenly aware of all sorts of emotions vibrating through him. Without meaning to, Sean found himself acutely conscious of every single part of the woman. At the same time, every shred of his own desire was making itself known to him.

It was as if he was attempting to put a lid on a pot that was threatening to explode at any second.

In that one moment in time, their eyes met, and suddenly, there were no more secrets between them, no more hiding places where those same unvoiced secrets could be tucked away.

The very intense desire that seemed to have been there right from the start took over, ready to govern her every move, her every thought.

January had never felt like this before, whether because she hadn't had any time, or because she had never been attracted to another man to this extent, she didn't know. All she did know was that whatever this was was threatening to explode within her, drenching every part of her, promising to be exquisite when it finally emerged.

She couldn't put any of this into words, and when she did try, Sean gently placed his finger against her lips, letting her know that right now, words really weren't necessary.

"We don't want to disturb her," he told her softly, nodding toward the sleeping Maya.

January still wasn't sure if they were on the same page, even though something—some deep inner instinct—told her that they were.

For now, January just took the hand that Sean offered her and followed him out of the room.

Without saying a word, as if talking at this moment

would somehow break the spell, Sean took January into his bedroom.

Looking around the room, January couldn't help smiling.

"You made your bed," she noted, although the rest of the room still looked like a hurricane had recently touched down, then left.

His eyes smiled at her as he said, "You're rubbing off on me." Then, because he was aware of what the rest of the room still looked like, he added with an appealing smile, "A little."

"Hey, Rome wasn't built in a day—or cleaned up in one, either," she told the man who had managed to totally hijack her heart without any effort whatsoever.

Every part of her smiled at him even as he began undoing her by slow, languid increments.

"No," Sean agreed, his voice low, husky, as he pressed a kiss to her throat. "It wasn't. But it's always good to have something to aspire to," he said, touching soft, tantalizing kisses along first one side of her neck and then the other.

Her pulse quickened and she could feel her knees being reduced to the consistency of well-cooked spaghetti, all but dissolving beneath her.

January found herself all but gasping for air. She dug her fingertips into his shoulders in an effort to remain upright.

He could feel her swaying against him, trying to regain her balance. "Am I going too fast?" Sean asked.

It took her a moment to actually comprehend the

words. What she was really aware of was the feel of his warm breath along her skin as he formed them.

Pulling herself together in order to focus on what he was actually asking, she finally answered, "No, not fast enough."

Her response pleased him, but at the same time, he wanted to be absolutely sure that she was a willing participant. That he hadn't somehow managed to overwhelm her so she couldn't think clearly. He needed this to be real.

With what seemed like lightning speed, this woman had become incredibly important to him and he didn't want to risk losing her because he had given in to the moment and, in so doing, had robbed her of her free will. He wanted her more than he could possibly say, but not that way.

"You're sure?" he asked.

January drew back just a little so that she could look at him. The detective made her feel almost dizzy, she realized—and she reveled in the sensation.

"Detective, I can sign a sworn statement to that effect if that would make you feel better, but could it wait until later?" Standing up on her toes, she brought her mouth up to less than an inch away from his. "Because right now, my hands have got better things to do than write," January assured Sean just before she pressed her lips against his.

Hard.

At the same time, she managed to undo Sean's belt, slipping it out of the loop that was holding it in place.

She felt his grin forming beneath her lips. "Multi-tasking?" Sean asked her.

There was nothing short of a wicked expression in her eyes as she answered, "Always."

She wasn't sure if, in the end, it was he or she who slid his trousers down his very taut, appealing hips. January was only aware that the garment was no longer an obstacle.

And neither was her dress.

Sean had sent hot shivers down her back as he slowly lowered the zipper. But the way her dress managed to all but sigh as it fell to the floor, no longer creating any sort of barrier between them, remained a mystery.

January wasn't interested in the why, only in the end result. And the end result was that very, very quickly they went from being dressed to being naked. They were cloaked only in red-hot desire. It was coupled with a network of pulse-scrambling kisses mutually pressed to every conceivable place on their throbbing bodies with superb results.

January had never even entertained an inkling of the fact that she could actually feel this beautiful, this overwhelmed. This incredibly exquisite. Accustomed to giving, she desperately wanted to share this wondrous feeling, to make Sean feel exactly what she was experiencing at this very moment. She could honestly say that every single part of her body was smiling and cheering at the same time.

While she had no idea exactly what was happening to her, she did know that she didn't want this to end—even though it had to.

Still, January tried to hang on to the mind-blowing sensation that had suddenly taken hold of her.

Sean felt his breath growing shorter and shorter. Like a man who had fallen overboard and was only marginally able to swim, he found himself close to being overwhelmed.

He never would have guessed, not in a million years, that this sweet, kind, thoughtful person he had impulsively kissed harbored a powerful storm within her. A storm that stirred his blood and made him unbelievably happy to be here with her tonight. This unexpected surprise completely took his breath away and made him want to pleasure her within an inch of both their lives.

Maybe it was foolish, but Sean couldn't shake the feeling that what was happening right at this moment was something that two people had never experienced before. Not to this extent.

It wasn't conceit or vanity that made him feel this way, just a secret insight that had taken over and was now, inexplicably, holding the reins.

Every kiss between them gave birth to one more. Every eager caress cloned itself into yet another, more stirring touch.

Heaven help him, but he couldn't seem to get enough even as he tried his very best not to overwhelm her.

Or scare her off.

When he heard her labored breathing, he drew his head back, concerned. Had he gotten too carried away?

"Are you all right?" he asked, his eyes sweeping over her face.

"If I were any more all right," January told him, her eyes shining, "I'd probably be in heaven right about now."

Sean laughed then, relieved as well as delighted at the way she had assessed the situation.

"How do you know that this isn't heaven?" he asked. "Because it is, for me."

Then he filled his hands with her, bringing her body closer to his and exulting in every warm, giving inch of it as he caressed her.

He slowly kissed her over and over again, feasting on her lips before moving down to the swell of her breasts, thriving on the sounds of ecstasy that escaped her as she reacted to him.

When he found that he couldn't hold himself in check any longer, Sean laced his fingers through hers and drew himself up along her body.

January shivered in anticipation.

And then, his eyes on hers, Sean slowly entered her. The rhythm between them seemed to come on its own, filling his soul as well as hers.

Sean began to move.

At first it was just ever so slowly, but then the tempo increased. January matched it, moving with him beat for beat. She managed to delight him and tantalize him without even knowing it.

Sean kissed her harder as he continued to up the tempo until it was all but a frenzy throbbing between them.

Bound together in this inner paradise, they went faster and faster until they raced together as one to the very highest pinnacle on the summit.

The explosion that seized them echoed through their bodies simultaneously. They clung to each other, savoring the experience and wishing that it would never end, even though they knew that it would.

The euphoria melted away in layers, eventually leaving them in each other's arms, in awe of the moment and savoring the memory.

January felt her heart pounding so hard she thought it would stop. She waited for it to regain its normal rhythm.

It took a little longer for her to steady her breathing.

"Detective," January finally managed to say to him in a voice that was barely above a whisper. "You definitely have some hidden talents."

"That would probably be thanks to my earlier undercover work," he said wryly, kissing the top of her head as he held her close against him. "And you. Let's not forget you." He returned the compliment. "You are a total revelation."

"You mean I'm not the boring dud you thought I might be?" January asked, amused, as she continued to try to catch her breath.

Sean's grin grew wider. "The words *dud* or *boring* never crossed my mind. Give me a few minutes to regroup and I'll be ready for round two."

Not that she wasn't sorely tempted, but she knew she couldn't give in to that. And she told him as much. "Oh, as enticing as that really is, I think that might be pushing it."

Sean raised himself up on his elbow to look at her. "Don't tell me I drained you," he said incredulously. The way she moved, Sean was convinced that the woman had enough energy to go on like that indefinitely.

"No, it's not that," she told him with more than a tinge of regret in her voice. "But I feel like I should be getting back to the guest room before Maya wakes up and wonders where I am. She's much too young to understand what happened here, and on top of that, I never learned the proper signs to explain to her what we just did—even if I wanted to, which I really don't," January added with feeling.

Getting off his bed, she looked around for her discarded clothes while Sean caught himself looking at her—and aching for her all over again.

"Yeah, maybe you'd better go," he reluctantly agreed. "Before I totally disregard all the sense you're making and give in to this overwhelming desire to seduce you."

"Seduce me?" January echoed, amused, as she pulled on her dress. Since she was going back to bed once she reached the guest room, she didn't put on any of her undergarments. "Is that what you call it?" she asked him. "Because from where I was, it looked pretty much like we were seducing each other."

Sitting up on the bed, Sean reached over and hooked his arm around her waist, pulling her to him. He was unable to resist one last, deep kiss.

Releasing her after several beats, Sean took in a long breath. "Yeah," he agreed with a grin. "I guess you're right." Nodding his head, he allowed his eyes to wash over her one last time. "We're going to need to talk about that."

She looked at him, uncertainty undulating through

her. Why did he want to talk about it? Was he already beginning to regret what had happened tonight? She had next to no experience with men, but she knew a lot of women who had poured out their hearts to her, telling her about being tossed aside after having what they thought was the perfect romantic interlude. They had thought they were building something when it turned out they had experienced the vibrations of a death knell.

"Why would you want to talk about it?" she asked, even as she warned herself to drop the subject.

"Well, I don't know about you, but after what just happened between us, I really don't want that to be the last time," Sean told her.

As he talked, Sean quickly got dressed again. All he could think of was that Maya might accidentally come looking for them. He didn't want her education to take a turn for the adult at this point in her life.

January blinked, staring at him. Did he just say what she thought he had, or was that purely wishful thinking on her part?

"You don't?" she asked him.

"No, I don't," he answered with emphasis, then asked her pointedly, "Do you?"

She stared at him. "Would I be too pushy if I said no, I don't?"

"I'm sorry, my head's a little scrambled," he admitted. "Is that no, you don't want it to be the last time, or no, you—"

She leaned over and stopped his mouth with her own. It was the best way she knew to end this line of conversation that seemed likely to go around in circles and not lead to the desired destination.

When she stopped kissing him this time, January told him, "No, at the risk of sounding like a complete pushover, I do *not* want this to be the last time you and I build our own stairway to heaven."

He grinned. "That is a very interesting way to put it."

"Well, right now, that is the only way I am going to be able to put it. I've really got to get back to Maya before she wakes up, gets scared and comes looking for me."

"She might *not* wake up," he told her.

"Maybe not," January agreed, "but I really don't want to risk it."

"Yeah." Sean nodded, even though it cost him. "You really shouldn't."

Her mouth dropped open at the same time that her heart swelled. The words escaped her mouth before she could react to stop them.

"And that's why I love you."

The next moment, she was stunned as shock—not to mention instant regret—filled her. January had no idea what had come over her. She had allowed words that should never have seen the light of day emerge, unencumbered, on their own.

Chapter 19

She realized that attempting to backtrack at this point wasn't going to do her any good.

"I mean—" January had no idea how to take back what she had just said.

Sean could only look at her, speechless, because of what he had just heard her say. "You what?"

"Nothing," January cried, unable to take it back and at the same time very aware that she was attempting to close the barn door a second after the horse had managed to gallop off, escaping. "I'm delirious," she quipped. "I don't know what I'm saying."

"Well, from here it sounded like you said you loved me," Sean told her. The expression on his face was totally serious.

Tossing her head, January tried her best to brazen

it out. "If I were you, I'd get my hearing checked," she informed him, avoiding his eyes as she headed for the bedroom door.

"It's good to know," Sean continued, ignoring her disclaimer and commenting on what January had just said.

"And why's that?" she asked without turning around.

"Because," he replied very matter-of-factly, "I think I love you, too."

That statement, uttered without any fanfare, stopped her dead in her tracks. It took her a minute to recapture her breath. Very slowly, she turned to look at Sean, then she immediately turned back toward the hallway.

This was just too much for her to deal with, January thought.

"I've got to get back to Maya," she said, her voice all but stilted.

Sean nodded as if they were having a regular conversation. He wasn't about to stop her from leaving. Instead, he casually told her, "I'll put this on the list of things we need to talk about."

January made no comment. She just continued down the hallway.

Still, she couldn't get herself to stop smiling.

He needed to get his mind off January and back on the reason he was here in the first place, Sean upbraided himself. His priority was protecting Maya. But he was also focused on finding a way to bring down Mercer. He needed to find out if the drug lord was the one who had executed those three men in the warehouse, or if he'd paid someone to do it for him.

Sean's search for answers hadn't led him anywhere, but he wasn't about to give up. His gut told him that there had to be something that he was missing.

It had to be somewhere in his records, he thought. He just needed to find what it was that he had managed to somehow overlook.

His thoughts kept him up for most of the remainder of the night.

He finally managed to drift off. And when he did wake up, it was to the warm, tempting smell of fried eggs and bacon.

January was making breakfast, he realized.

A man could really get used to this.

Throwing off the covers, the detective took a five-minute shower then quickly got dressed. He was making his way to the kitchen within ten minutes after opening his eyes.

Because of the aroma, Sean had expected to find January in the kitchen, preparing breakfast. But he was surprised that she had a pint-sized assistant helping her. The chord that this utterly domestic scene struck made him smile.

"Is she really helping?" he asked, nodding at Maya. "Or does she get underfoot?"

January hadn't heard Sean entering and, remembering last night in all its glorious detail, she smiled warmly at him.

"Let's just say that she's *learning* how to help," January answered. "But she's not really getting underfoot. She is helping." Changing the topic slightly, she asked him, "How do you want your eggs this morning?"

He suddenly realized that he was so hungry, preparation didn't matter. "Cooked," he answered simply.

January could feel her eyes crinkling at the corners. She was trying very hard to divorce herself from this euphoria that had seized her soul, but it was extremely hard to achieve that impartial distance.

"You really are very easy," January told the detective.

Sean nodded, doing his best to look serious. "I try to be," he replied, looking at Maya. He smiled at the little girl before he signed a greeting to her.

January brought over Sean's plate and placed it in front of him. Since he hadn't asked for anything special, she gave him the sunny-side-up eggs she had already prepared.

"You just said good morning to her," January observed, stunned and impressed.

Sean nodded. "I know what I said," he replied, smiling at Maya.

January wasn't ready to let the subject go. "You're really getting good with that," she said, commenting on the way he had taken to signing.

"The internet is a great source of information on just about everything," he told her. "I just decided to look up a few terms after you went to bed last night." His eyes met hers. "I couldn't sleep."

January's delighted smile seemed to encompass her entire face. "I could," she told him. "As a matter of fact, I slept like a baby."

He considered that for a moment, then shrugged. "Not sure just what that says about me," Sean admitted.

A wicked twinkle entered her eyes. "I guess we'll just have to figure it out as we go along," she told him. "But for now, eat your breakfast." January pointed at his plate. "You need to keep up your strength."

Though he was trying to separate himself from last night's events, he wasn't quite as successful as he would have liked to be. "I certainly will if I plan to share another go-round with you any time in the near future."

Anticipation undulated through her and her grin grew that much more wicked.

"We'll see," January told him. Finishing her breakfast, she moved back her plate. "So, what do you have on tap for today?"

His answer would sound deadly dull to her, he thought. "I've got to get some work done on my ongoing investigation," Sean told her, then anticipated her next question. "And yes, I'll check with the lab to see if they've managed to make any progress with finding a match on Maya's DNA test."

January remained seated for another minute or so. "Nice to know you're on top of things," she told him.

Maya had scooted into her seat earlier, sitting down opposite Sean. She was watching him with adoring eyes and for all the world appeared to be absorbing each of his words, even though January knew that was really impossible.

Listening to January, it was Sean's turn to smile wickedly at her. "I guess I have my moments," the detective admitted.

* * *

"That was a really great breakfast," he told January less than fifteen minutes later. His plate was completely denuded of every last morsel of food. "Want help with the dishes?" he offered.

Smiling, January shook her head. "You'll just get in the way. Maya and I will handle what's here. Go, do your thing," she told him, waving the detective off. "Make the world safe."

Sean rose to his feet. "Never let it be said that I ignored a lady." He gave her a formal salute and winked at Maya. "I'll be in my office if you need me—and even if you don't," he added whimsically, then left.

Try as he might, he kept coming to the same dead end time after time, Sean thought. He was staring at the same array of photographs depicting Kid Mercer at different stages of his notorious career.

"What the hell am I missing, Mercer?" he demanded of the subject of all these photographs. "And just where did you disappear to? Was that why you killed those three men? Because one of them could tell me where to find you?"

Sean flipped through the various images, feeling frustrated and utterly stymied. "Too many questions, not enough answers," he complained to the cartel leader who wasn't there.

Sean was so immersed in looking through the drug lord's file, he didn't hear Maya come in at first. He had deliberately left his study door open to get a little air circulating through the tiny room. Otherwise, with his computer running, the small bedroom/study became much too warm all too quickly, even though it was still winter.

Seeing the shadow cast over his computer, Sean looked up. And smiled.

"Hi, princess," he said, greeting her even though he knew Maya couldn't hear him. He reasoned that talking to her somehow comforted him. "I'm a little busy right now. Maybe I can play with you later," he suggested.

Maya cocked her head, making him think of a bird that was trying to understand what a human was saying. It was frustrating for him. Sean wanted to be able to communicate with her, to get the basic gist of what he wanted to say across to her.

"Bear with me, princess. I'm not very good at this yet," Sean said as he did his best to sign at least a little of what he had just said.

Maya stood by his desk, watching him with wide, patient eyes. He had the feeling that at least a part of her felt sorry for him.

That was okay, he thought. Sympathy acted in his favor.

But as he awkwardly tried to tell her that he would play with her as soon as he had done a little more of his work, Sean watched as Maya's eyes suddenly grew very large.

"I sure hope that I didn't just say something I shouldn't have," he told her, knowing his words were only a comfort to him, not her.

It took him a second to realize that Maya wasn't focused on him anymore. She was looking at one of the photographs he had pulled up on his computer screen. Guilt shot through Sean.

She shouldn't be looking at those, he thought. The man on the screen was a killer. He was—

Maya had suddenly grown very excited, shifting from foot to foot and signing the same word over and over again.

The third time she did it, Sean realized that he recognized what she was signing—or thought he did.

Stunned, he heard himself asking Maya, "Did you just sign *daddy*?"

That was the first word he had seen her signing. It couldn't be a coincidence.

"January," he called out, raising his voice. "Can you come in here, please?"

A minute later, January came into the room, drying her hands on the dish towel she had slung over her shoulder.

"Sorry," she apologized. "I didn't realize that Maya had come in here, looking for her idol. I'll just take her to—"

Sean waved away her apology. "I think Maya just signed *daddy*." Raising his eyes to January, he said, "I think that Kid Mercer might be Maya's father." He grew more excited as he entertained the possibility. "You know what that means, don't you?"

Not waiting for January to answer, he told her his theory. "Those men we thought were after Maya weren't after her to *kill* her because she was a witness. They were trying to kidnap her in order to bring her back to Mercer. She's his daughter. Look at how excited Maya got recognizing him." He pointed to the little girl's face. "She's too innocent to be devious. Mercer has to be her father." The moment he'd said that, Sean took out his cell phone.

"Are you calling the lab?" January asked Sean.

He nodded, repeating the words and confirming her suspicions. "Calling the lab."

The moment Sean got through, he told the CSI tech who picked up to compare the DNA sample he had brought in to Mercer's DNA that was on file. He asked the tech to get back to him as quickly as possible.

Hanging up, he looked at Maya, still somewhat surprised. "Who would have ever thought Kid Mercer was your daddy?" he marveled.

January, meanwhile, had arrived at her own decision about this situation. "She can't go back to him," she told Sean flatly. When he looked at her quizzically, she said, "I don't care if he is her father." She was not about to be argued out of the stand she had taken. "Maya obviously loves him, but it's not safe for her to be with him. I am not about to allow her to go back to live with a killer."

The man had to understand why she was taking this position. "Think of what could happen to her," she said emphatically, shaking her head. "No, there has to be another way."

While they were talking, Maya had gone up to the computer, spreading her fingers out over Mercer's image as if she could actually *feel* his skin beneath her fingers.

Observing her, January could only shake her head. "Breaks your heart. Some people just don't deserve the love that they get. That DNA test," she asked, turning toward Sean, "can it help us to locate her mother?"

"Yes, if the woman is in the system for any reason," he told January, then added an all-important qualification. "And if she's still alive."

"We need to get Maya into protective custody," January argued. Especially if they couldn't identify her mother.

But Sean shook his head. "Mercer will find her," he predicted. "Mercer's good. He's got feelers out everywhere. It'll just be a matter of time before he finds her."

"All right, so how do you propose we keep her safe?" January asked belligerently.

"Well, I've got an idea," he told her.

She could have sworn a chill shot up and down her spine. Her eyes met his. "I'm not about to risk Maya's life by using her as bait," January informed him.

"Dabbling in mind reading?" he asked her.

Her eyes narrowed. She had her answer. "Then you *are* planning on using her as bait." What was he thinking? "You can't do that," she told the detective. "I won't let you."

"Relax, tiger, I'm not going to use her as bait, not really," he clarified. "I am using the *thought* of her as bait."

She stared at him, shaking her head. "You're going to have to make that a little clearer for me."

"I will," Sean promised, adding, "All in due time. But first, to set this plan in motion, I'm going to need to get in contact with that so-called new 'chef' your sister Tatum hired."

Her eyes narrowed as she tried to make sense out of what Sean was saying. Where was he going with this? Unfortunately, he had managed to completely lose her.

"I said clearer, not muddier," January reminded him.

He told her as much as he was free to share. "I need to call Cruz," he told her. "And then call in a few favors. In order to assure ourselves that Maya remains safe, we are going to need to set a trap for Mercer. If he takes the bait, we can get him permanently off the streets."

"And you can do this without putting Maya's life in any sort of jeopardy?" January asked, never taking her eyes off his face. She hated this plateau they had suddenly reached, but the little girl's life depended on her being careful.

That meant not blindly following Sean just because she had fallen in love with him.

"Trust me. When I'm finished setting this trap, she's never going to be in danger again," he told the worried woman beside him. Seeing the doubt in her eyes, Sean said, "You're going to have to trust me, January."

January sighed. She knew he was right. Even so, she knew she had to ask, "Do I have a choice?"

Sean's eyes met hers. "Ideally, no."

"Well, then I guess I trust you," January said, resigned. "Let me get hold of Cruz for you," she offered.

"I'd appreciate that," Sean responded, already taking out his cell phone to make another call to someone at the police station.

Chapter 20

"You wanted to see me?" Cruz Medina asked, closing the door behind him as he slipped into Tatum Colton's office at the rear of True Restaurant.

He was on his break, which he judged was the perfect time to meet with the man he knew was a Homicide detective. The same man he had just run into at the Coltons' house during the family gathering.

"Yes," Sean replied, gesturing toward a chair facing Tatum's desk. Cruz chose to stand. Sean took it as a sign. The undercover detective was leery.

"Look, why don't we just spare ourselves the needless dancing around the facts," Sean suggested.

Cruz looked at him blankly. "I'm not sure what you're talking about."

Sean could appreciate the man being careful, but

right now, he didn't have time for this. "Then let me explain it to you," he said flatly. "Your current partner used to be my old partner when he worked in Homicide. Before he switched over to the Narcotics Division. You can call and ask him." He knew that was taking a chance, after how he and Harry had parted, but he trusted his former partner to vouch for him.

"All right," Cruz replied vaguely, neither confirming nor denying Sean's assumption. Taking quiet measure of the man before him, Cruz sat down. "So where is this thing going?"

"I need to have someone plant some information for Elias 'Kid' Mercer to 'uncover,'" Sean told Cruz without any preamble.

"What kind of information?" Cruz asked, eyeing Sean suspiciously.

In an ideal world, he would have been able to work his way up to this, feeling Cruz out as he went. But the world he found himself in was far from ideal.

Okay, here goes everything. "I want it known that his daughter, Maya, is being moved to a safe house. Once we have her there, it's only a matter of time before she's going to be put into witness protection. He'll never see her again."

"Maya," Cruz repeated. An image immediately clicked in his head. "You mean that kid you brought with you to the party—"

"—is Mercer's daughter, yeah," Sean confirmed. "I thought that because she might have witnessed a triple murder, Mercer had sent out his people to eliminate her. Turns out I think he wants his people to bring her home to him." The more he thought about it, the more he believed that January had been right about Mercer. Daughter or no daughter, he couldn't be allowed to get his hands on Maya.

For his part, Cruz looked stunned. "How about that?" he cried. "I knew Mercer had a kid, but I thought she was older." He thought about the other fact he had learned, watching some of Tatum's family interact with the little girl. "And I definitely didn't know that she couldn't hear."

"Yeah." Sean nodded solemnly. "Changes the playing field, doesn't it?"

Cruz made no comment one way or the other. Something far more important had struck him. The social worker had seemed very protective toward the child in her care, more so than he would have thought was usual. "Is January okay with this?" he asked Sean, elaborating in case the detective didn't catch his meaning. "Using the kid as bait to catch the kid's father?"

"The story we're putting out is the bait," Sean corrected him. "The little girl definitely isn't."

That sounded like a pretty gray area to Cruz. "Someday, you're gonna have to explain that, but right now—" he glanced at his watch "—I've got to be getting back.

"And don't worry, I'll see to it that this 'information' winds up on the streets." He had one question for Sean. "Your end game is to lock up that SOB, right?"

"Right," Sean confirmed. "I want to lock Mercer up and not only throw away the key, but weld the door permanently shut."

"Okay, then count me in," Cruz said, surrendering the last of the pretense he had cloaked himself in. For the first time since he had entered the office, he grinned. "Damn, that means I can finally ditch this undercover gig and start living a normal life again."

Sean couldn't help but laugh. "You call what we do for a living *normal*?"

To Cruz there was no question about that. "You mean in comparison to this dual life?" he asked, gesturing around Tatum's office. He had come to Tatum's restaurant for a specific reason. He was here pretending to be a drug dealer who in turn was pretending to be a chef. There were times when he felt himself dangerously close to losing track of all the pretenses that were involved. "Hell, yes," Cruz said with enthusiasm.

Sean had done his homework, looking into the reason that would have brought an undercover agent to Tatum's door in the first place. The answer was more than a little surprising.

"You really think that Tatum's restaurant is laundering drug cartel money?" Sean asked the dark-haired pseudo-chef bluntly.

Cruz shrugged noncommittally. "I can only go with the evidence," he answered.

"But you don't believe it," Sean guessed, reading between the lines.

"What I believe doesn't matter," Cruz told Sean.

Sean knew better. Every good law enforcement agent he had ever met relied heavily on their own gut feelings. And he had a feeling that Cruz's gut exonerated Tatum.

Wanting to get away from this line of conversation, Cruz repeated, "I'll make sure the word about Maya's safe house gets spread around. We'll see if that gets the big fish to bite."

Sean rose to his feet. He had another appointment to get to. "I'm counting on it—for everyone's sake," he said as he left Tatum's office.

Sean's next—and last—stop before he went back to January and Maya was the police station. If everything went according to plan—meaning that he would wind up taking down Mercer—Sean knew he would need backup.

Since, technically, taking down Mercer and his associates was the province of the Narcotics Division, that division would be the one that he needed to approach for backup if his plan were to be pulled off. Under perfect conditions, he could go in, make the necessary arrangements and then get back out again in a matter of minutes.

But conditions, Sean had learned almost from the start of his law enforcement career, were never ideal. In this case that meant that, preoccupied the way he was with the myriad details involved in catching Mercer, he was not in the best frame of mind to run into Harry Cartwright.

Which was exactly what happened. Murphy's Law was alive and well.

His path and Harry's crossed almost immediately. Had he *wanted* this, Sean thought, he definitely couldn't have pulled it off any better.

Standing by the elevator on the first floor, Sean had just pressed the up button when an old, familiar voice coming from behind him said, "Hi, stranger. How's everything going?"

Recognition was immediate. He didn't even have to think about it.

He knew in his heart that this wasn't the time or the place to have this conversation, but since he didn't know when the next time might come up—if ever—this, by default, *was* the right time and place.

Turning around to face his former partner, Sean pasted a smile on his lips. "Hi, Harry. It's been a long time."

"Two years," Harry acknowledged. The six-foot detective had lost some weight and had gained a beard, Sean noted.

"I know," Sean replied. Since he *had* run into his former partner, there was no way for him to remain aloof. "And I've been aware of every single hour of every single one of those days." It was now or never, he thought. He really needed to get this off his conscience. "Harry, I just want to tell you one more time how very sorry I am for what happened to your wife and daughter."

Having started this, he just kept going. "The amount of guilt I've been carrying around because I wasn't able to get there in time to save them almost crushed me," Sean solemnly admitted. "And I *never* meant for what happened to them to wind up chasing you away." Sean felt as if he had suffered a double loss, losing what he had considered to be his secondary family, and because of that, he had lost his best friend.

"Chasing me away?" Harry repeated, bewildered. "Is that why you think I left?"

"Well, didn't you? Because you blamed me for not being able to get there in time to protect them? Trust me, I've lived with that guilt every day for the last two years."

"Then stop blaming yourself," Harry ordered. "Because I don't."

I don't believe that, Sean thought. "If that were true, then why did you get a transfer?" He didn't believe Harry's protestations.

"I didn't get a transfer because of you," Harry told him. "I got a transfer because I needed a fresh start. I wanted to be around people who didn't have pity in their eyes every time they looked at me. There's just so much silence a man can endure when he enters a room. Hell, it was bad enough that I was pitying myself. I didn't need to have that reinforced a dozen times a day because of the people I encountered."

Sean could see his point. And it was a total relief to know that his old friend didn't hold him responsible for what had happened.

"So how are you doing?" Sean asked. They hadn't talked in those two years. There was a lot to catch up on once this whole episode was in his rearview mirror.

Harry shrugged, not certain where to begin. "Well, it's been over two years and I've started to move on—I think," he added a little hesitantly.

Sean thought of the women he had met at January's parents' house. "If you're interested in testing the waters, just say the word. My girl has a couple of single sisters and a female cousin who are nothing short of knockouts. I'm sure I can get you fixed up with any one of them."

Harry looked stunned, but not for the reason that Sean would have assumed. "Hey, hold it a second. Back up."

"You don't want to get fixed up?" Sean guessed, thinking that maybe he had gotten his signals confused.

"No, it's not that." Harry quickly denied that idea. "*My girl*?" he repeated quizzically. "You have a girl? Since when?"

"Well, I haven't exactly been living under a rock," Sean protested. He didn't have time to go into that now, but he definitely would, he promised himself.

Harry laughed. The elevator arrived and they both got on. For now, they had the car to themselves. "The Sean Stafford I knew had a permanent residence under a rock. As I recall, you were always saying you were too busy to socialize." Harry grinned at him. "Congratulations for coming out from under that rock and finally joining the living."

"Does that mean you want me to fix you up?" Sean asked.

"That means that when this is finally over," Harry said, referring to what Cruz had told him was going on, "and we have that rat-bastard Mercer behind bars, we can give it a try. But for now, tell me what you're involved in and just how much backup you think you're going to need."

"Does the word *army* bring an image to mind?" Sean asked.

The elevator stopped and opened its doors. Harry put

his hand on Sean's back, ushering him out. "Why don't we go see my lieutenant and you can tell him what you need?" Harry urged.

"Sounds like a good idea," Sean agreed, following his old partner.

"I don't like it," Sean declared.

After his meeting with the lieutenant at Narcotics Division, he had come home to tell January that all the pieces looked to be in place and his proposed plan was a go.

That was when January had informed him that she was going to be at the safe house, as well.

She was not about to be talked out of it and dug in. "Sean, if I'm not there, this guy is immediately going to be suspicious. If he gets word of it, he might not even show up." She saw the expression on his face. Sean was definitely resisting the idea. "In order to sell this, I *need* to be there. Mercer is not stupid. He's not going to believe that I let his daughter out of my sight, not after everything that's gone down."

"I don't like you taking chances like this," Sean said with feeling.

"I appreciate your concern, Sean," she replied patiently, touched at where he was coming from. After all, he was worried about her. "But it's not up to you. It's up to me. I'm the only one who gets to vote on this and I vote yes. Like you said, this is the only way that we will ever be rid of Mercer. Rid of the threat he represents to her—and to me. I want to be able to sleep again, Sean."

Sean shook his head. He only had himself to blame.

He had inadvertently pulled her into this. "You know, I should have never told you anything."

"Too late," January said. "You did," she told him, adding, "Now let's move on from there. By the way, where is this safe house?"

"Not all that far from here," Sean said, reluctant to disclose the exact address until the time came. He still looked rather dubious about having her take up residence in the safe house. "Are you sure I can't talk you out of staying there?" He had no idea when Mercer was going to show up at the house. Most likely when they least expected it. "You know you would make my job a whole lot easier if you just go where I tell you to."

"What fun is that?" she asked innocently. And then January became serious. "You know I'm right, Sean. And besides, what safer place for me to be than in the heart of a police operation?"

"Any one of a dozen places," he answered. "Maybe two dozen."

"Why Detective Stafford," she cried, blinking her eyelashes at him in double time. "I never knew you to exaggerate."

"Desperate times call for desperate measures," he told her.

"So now you're desperate?" January asked, amused.

His eyes met hers. "Now I'm a lot of things I never was before."

But even as he said it, he knew there was no talking her out of this and he would be lying if a part of him, albeit a very small part, didn't admit that her feisty spirit was one of the things that he loved about her. The only thing he worried about was that that same feisty spirit would wind up getting her into trouble that neither one of them was prepared for.

"Don't worry," she told him, brushing her lips against his in a quick, affectionate kiss. "I'm not going to take any unnecessary chances."

"That doesn't exactly comfort me," he told her, "because the way you think, you probably see a lot of chances as being necessary."

January laughed, tickled. "You, Detective Stafford, have just got to stop peeking into my diary. A woman needs to have some secrets."

He was not amused right now. He was worried. "A woman needs to remain alive in order to have those secrets."

They were getting nowhere, and she didn't want to keep going around in circles. "We are going to argue this into the ground, Sean. Let's just agree to disagree— and let me go ahead with your plan," she told him.

He had an alternate idea. "I could just tie you up and leave you in the closet," Sean suggested.

But January was not about to budge. Mentally, she was already living in a world where all this was behind her, and she wasn't about to give that up.

"You could try," she told him. "But I promise you, it's not going to be easy—and there'll be bite marks and bruising," she added with a confident smile.

Sean shook his head as he slipped an arm around her shoulders and drew her closer to him. "You are one hell of a handful," he told her.

January saw no reason to argue. "I am," she agreed, then said with a smile, "And I'm all yours."

"Lucky me," he commented.

The corners of her mouth curved just as her eyes joined in on the smile. "And don't you forget it," she told him.

"Me? Forget the best thing that ever happened to me?" he asked innocently. "I wouldn't dare. All right, if you're determined to go through with this, are you ready?" he asked, even as he told himself he shouldn't be doing this.

"Detective, I was *born* ready," she said, just as her heart began to pound.

"That," he responded grimly, "is exactly what I'm afraid of." He looked at the screen on his phone and read the text that had just come in. His backup team was in place. "Okay, get 'Maya' and let's do this," he said.

Chapter 21

Sean was beginning to think that this whole safe-house setup had been a bad idea.

It had been two days now since "Maya" and January moved into the safe house. At some point, the real Maya would be permanently transferring to another state and another identity.

Two days and there had been no unwanted visitors.

No visitors at all, Sean thought, feeling restless. The only one who had come by in all that time was a delivery boy from a local supermarket. That had been on the first full day that residency had been set up.

Sean was really becoming antsy, not to mention that his body was cramping up. Except for a few hours when one of the Narcotics detectives had taken over the watch—Sean had slept in the back seat of the car then—Sean had remained on duty and on his guard the entire time.

If something didn't happen soon, like by tomorrow, he would be sorely tempted to just pack it all in. Admittedly, this plan had been a shot in the dark, and like so many of those, Sean thought ruefully, it had hit nothing.

It looked as if, he decided, they would have to find some other way to bring down the drug cartel chieftain.

But what?

Sean had been banking on Mercer's attachment to his flesh and blood to reel him in. What else could be used to motivate—

Sean sat up straighter. He was positive that he had heard a noise. When all of this had been set up, a sophisticated version of a baby monitor had been put in the living room and another one was placed in the bedroom where January was staying with Maya. He had quickly become attuned to all the normal noises in the house and this particular noise definitely wasn't normal, he thought.

Every single bone in his body told him that someone who shouldn't be was in the house.

Scanning the area, Sean tried to zero in on something that didn't belong. A car parked where it shouldn't have been, someone walking their dog who normally wasn't out at this time. Two people taking an evening stroll.

But nothing was out of place.

That didn't mean that there wasn't something amiss, Sean thought.

"Hey Donavan, are you hearing this?" he asked Donavan, talking into a walkie-talkie to one of the officers who was staked out in a vehicle a block away.

There was no answer.

That wasn't good, Sean thought.

Feeling uneasy, he decided not to bother checking in with January. He would go to the house and scope things out for himself.

But even as he got out of the car and began to head for the safe house, he heard January's voice. There was an edge to it.

She was talking to someone, challenging them and enunciating clearly.

Sean knew that was for his benefit. He stepped up his pace.

"Who are you?" he heard January demanding angrily. "How did you get in? What are you doing here?"

"You ask too many questions, lady," a deep voice answered. "That's a quick way to wind up dead. Too bad no one ever taught you not to be so nosy."

Sean heard her ask, "What do you want?"

Damn it, January, stop trying to goad him, he thought, afraid for her.

"I'm here to claim what is mine," the man answered.

Mercer!

Sean was running now, but he still wasn't close enough to the safe house. He would have preferred using his car, but the sound of the approaching vehicle would have definitely tipped off the drug lord.

Sean had his phone in his hand.

He hit the conference call button, connecting with

all the other police officers staked out in the immediate area.

"Mercer's in the house. I repeat, Mercer's in the house. I need every available backup closing in *now*!" he said emphatically.

"I'd leave now if I were you," Sean heard January saying to her unwanted visitor.

Just stall, January, Sean thought. There was such a thing as being foolhardy and he was terrified that she had crossed that line.

"Not without my daughter!" he heard Mercer growl. It wasn't hard to envision the rest of the scenario.

As January held her breath and watched, Mercer made his way over to his daughter's bed. The drug lord pulled down Maya's covers so he could grab the little girl and make off with her.

For one frozen moment, Mercer stared at the uncovered figure in the bed, stunned.

"A doll?" he cried. "You put a *damn doll* in her bed?" Pure rage contorted the man's deeply tanned face. "Where is she?" he demanded. "You've got one chance to live. Tell me where she is! Maya!" he called out in frustration, searching for the little girl.

"Don't you know your daughter can't hear you?" January asked him in disbelief.

Mercer's face had darkened to the point that January found it frightening.

"I know that!" he screamed in her face. "Don't tell me about my daughter! She belongs with me!" The cartel leader raised his weapon, aiming his gun at January.

"Now where is she?" he demanded. "Tell me and I'll make this quick, otherwise—"

He didn't finish.

He didn't have to.

January was stalling, attempting to give Sean as much time as she could to get here. She knew he had to be listening—unless this monster had already done something to him, she suddenly thought.

Oh Lord, please let me be wrong, she prayed, afraid of where her thoughts were leading her. Sean had to be all right. He *had* to be.

Her eyes met the drug lord's. "If you really cared about your daughter, you'd give her up and let her live with someone who could give her a decent, normal life and help her live it."

Mercer sneered. "Same garbage that her mother tried to pull." He waved away the suggestion. "That didn't end well for her. Now this is *your last chance*. Tell me where my daughter is or you're going to suffer a very painful, slow death!" he threatened nastily.

"She's where you can't get her," January answered defiantly.

"Too bad for you." The cartel lord raised his weapon, ominously cocking it.

"Drop the gun, Mercer!" Sean declared. Weapon drawn and aimed, he made his way into the room.

January was so relieved, her knees almost buckled out from under her. She came as close as she ever had to collapsing. Only strength of will managed to keep her on her feet.

"Where *were* you?" she asked, quickly hurrying over to Sean's side of the room.

"I would have been here faster if you didn't lock the damn windows," he told her, trying not to give in to the frustration that had created for him. He caught the drug lord's movement out of the corner of his eye. "I said drop it!" he ordered. Sean cocked his weapon to bring his point home. "You're under arrest, Mercer. It's all over."

"The hell it is!" Mercer declared, discharging his weapon.

Anticipating what Mercer was about to do—he had a reputation for acting irrationally, another reason for the nickname Kid—Sean pushed January down to the floor and covered her body with his own as he exchanged gunfire with the cartel leader.

A wave of nausea seized January. She came very close to throwing up, but somehow, she managed to keep it all down.

She could feel her heart pounding in every part of her body.

It was all over in less than a minute, over even before backup had a chance to break in. Mercer was on the floor, a growing pool of blood forming around what appeared to be his lifeless body.

January scrambled to her feet. "Are you all right?" she cried, looking at Sean as she quickly took inventory of all the visible places on his body.

"Yeah," Sean started to answer her. "I think that I'm—"

"Sean!" January screamed as she saw the supposedly dead drug lord raising his gun. He was aiming it directly at Sean's back.

Alerted, Sean spun around and fired his weapon at Mercer again. Mercer's gun dropped out of his limp hand as the drug lord fell over again, this time totally immobile.

Not leaving anything to chance, Sean placed two fingers against the killer's neck and checked for himself. There was no pulse.

"He's finally dead," Sean told January. And then he smiled grimly at her. "You saved my life, January."

It was as if all the air had suddenly been drained out of her. She slumped against Sean, quietly sobbing. "You're welcome," she said, unable to still the quiver in her voice.

Sean spun around when he heard the door being opened, his weapon raised and ready.

"Hey." Donavan raised his hands. He looked relieved to find them both alive. "We come in peace," he quipped. Looking at the bloody scene, the detective said, "Looks to me like you two could really use some peace. What the hell happened?"

"Mercer had a completely different future in mind for his daughter than we did," Sean told the other detective.

Donavan nodded. "We got the three men he brought with him," he told Sean. "My guess is that they wanted to live more than their boss did." Donavan looked from Sean to the visibly shaken woman beside him. "You two okay?" he asked, concerned.

"Well, there're no bullet holes," Sean answered,

glancing first at January, then down at himself. "And with Mercer no longer presiding over his drug empire, I'd say that the rest of the situation is looking pretty good—at least for now." He knew that nothing remained permanent in the cartel world. He slipped his arm around January's shoulders. "I'm going to take January home. Tell your lieutenant I'll be there in the morning to file all the reports he needs."

Donavan nodded, a small smile curving his mouth. "That'll definitely make his day. But as for Mercer's drug empire, killing him is like cutting off the head of a hydra. No matter how hard you try to prevent it, another head is bound to pop up, and then it starts all over again."

"Yeah, I know," Sean agreed with a sigh. "But with any luck, there'll be some breathing space in between heads."

"We can only hope," Donavan said as he went to join the rest of his team to canvas the aftermath of the crime scene.

Sean looked back at January. "Are you ready to go home?"

It was a rhetorical question. He was taking her home whether she was ready or not. She looked drained and exhausted.

"Your home or mine?" she asked.

"You pick," he told her. This wasn't the time to pressure her in any way. She needed to feel like she had some sort of control over her life, however minor.

"Could we go to yours?" January asked. "I don't think I'm up to facing Maya yet. When I see her, I'm going to have to tell her that her daddy's dead." Her eyes filled with tears. "I need some time to figure out how to do that."

Before going to the safe house, they had left Maya back at January's town house. Both of her sisters and her cousin Carly were taking turns looking after the little girl. Because Maya seemed to have taken to all three of them, January felt she didn't have to worry about leaving the little girl with them, although she hadn't reckoned on being gone for so long.

And now, even though she wanted to go rushing back to see Maya—had it really been almost three days?—January knew she couldn't go, not until she had had a chance to get her thoughts organized so she could explain to Maya what had happened. She needed to use the calmest, most neutral manner she could to sign to the girl and explain why she wasn't going to be going back to her father.

"Maybe we can break it to her later," Sean suggested. "For now, until all this is ironed out, maybe one of us should think about adopting her." He looked at January, trying to read her expression. "Does that sound like it might be a possibility?"

"Yes, it is," she agreed, then said, "Although there is another possibility."

Sean's eyes met hers and he knew what she was suggesting—or at least he thought he did.

"We could adopt her together," Sean said.

Although that thought had been what she was entertaining, the moment she heard the words out loud, January knew that was what she wanted to do. Adopt Maya together with Sean.

But there was one problem with that standing in their way.

"They won't allow two single people to adopt her," she pointed out.

She was surprised to see Sean shaking his head. "Not a problem," he told her.

She wasn't going to question him about that. Or push his statement to its logical conclusion. She didn't want to be disappointed in case she was wrong.

For now, she was just going to take solace in the fact that they were both alive and that a horrible, horrible man no longer posed a threat to any of them. Most importantly, not to Maya.

Eventually, January fervently hoped, Maya would come to realize that, as well, and see that her life was actually so much better off without a narcissistic man in it. A man who made his living selling poison to anyone who could come up with the money to buy it, even if it meant that they would be committing their own horrible crimes in order to get it.

That thought, however, was far too wearying to contemplate right now. All she wanted to do, January thought, was to sink into Sean's arms and find comfort there.

He didn't even have to mean anything by it, she thought. All he had to do was just *be*. The rest of it, if there ever was going to be a rest of it, could take care of itself tomorrow.

Sean drove up to January's town house. Parking his vehicle directly in front, he got out and rounded the hood to get to the passenger side. He opened her door and put his hand out to her, silently indicating that she should take it.

When she did, he closed his fingers over hers, helping her out of her seat.

"Let's go inside," he told January. "You need your rest. You went through a lot today."

The smile she gave him was one that looked exceptionally weary. "So did you."

"Yes, but there's just one difference. It's my job. I deliberately signed on for it. You didn't." And then he smiled as he recalled, "Instead, you barged your way into it."

"You know why. I wanted the stage that we set to be believable," she told him quietly. "If I wasn't there, since Mercer knew I had custody of Maya, it wouldn't be believable. Besides," she said with a smile playing on her lips, "Not everyone can play 'pretend' effectively with a doll."

Sean blew out a breath. "I know, and I'm not about to argue with you over that," Sean told her. "The end result is that Maya is no longer in any sort of danger from her father or *because* of her father. And she has you to thank for that."

Still holding her hand, Sean slowly guided January to her front door. He waited for her to hand him the key to her town house. When she did, Sean put the key into the lock, disarmed the security system and opened the front door.

Once he ushered January inside, Sean rearmed the

security system, going through the motions in order to make her feel safe.

And once he was finished, then and only then did the detective who had fallen so deeply in love with her take January back into his arms and proceed to make her feel personally safe while holding her against him.

Chapter 22

The tall, dark-haired, willowy young woman had fire in her light brown eyes as she came storming into the police station a little more than thirty-six hours after Mercer's demise had become the news media's lead story.

"Is it true?" were the woman's opening words to the desk sergeant.

Sergeant Wallace Harrison had been selected for his present position because nothing flustered him. He looked now at the Latin whirlwind who had planted herself squarely in front of his desk. "Well, ma'am, you're going to have to be a little more specific than that," Harrison told her in a warm Southern drawl that had been known to disarm the most indignant of people.

Ruby Duarte took a deep breath, doing her best to

sound at least a little calmer. The dark-haired cashier with aspirations of becoming a nurse and who was presently enrolled in online courses toward that end attempted to appeal to the robust looking sergeant's best instincts. "The news bulletin on TV saying that Elias Mercer was killed yesterday while breaking into a safe house," she said as she tried to start from the beginning.

This was above the sergeant's pay grade to discuss. "Why don't I have you talk to one of the detectives involved in that case?" Harrison suggested.

Ruby was not about to be put off. "I don't want to talk to a detective," she cried. "I want to find out if my daughter was there."

"Your daughter?" the desk sergeant repeated, doing his best trying to follow her.

Despite her young age—she was twenty-four—Ruby Duarte was ordinarily a very quiet, reserved person. Mercer and his henchmen had used brute force to keep her from seeing Maya for years now. Not to be put off, she had come up with another plan. She had been secretly putting money aside and attempting to better herself. Her plan was to one day be able to steal her daughter away from the cartel drug lord.

"One day" had come sooner than Ruby had anticipated. She was eager to make it a reality before something else wound up separating her from her little girl. She was not going to put up with anything else keeping them apart.

"Yes!" Ruby declared, desperate to finally be reunited with Maya. "Someone told me that she was brought to this police station. Her name is Maya."

Maybe a description would shake up the desk sergeant's memory. "She's five years old and she's hearing impaired. I need to see her," Ruby cried. "Please."

A light went off in his head and the desk sergeant nodded. The pieces were all beginning to come together. Harrison knew who she was talking about. "You wait right here," he told the frantic young mother, getting on the phone. He put in a call to the Narcotics Division.

"Yeah, hi," he said to the detective who answered. "This is Sergeant Harrison at the front desk. Is Detective Stafford still up there?" He was given an affirmative answer. "Great. Would you ask him to come down to my desk? There's someone here claiming to be that little girl's mother. Right."

Hanging up, Harrison looked at the distraught young woman in front of him. "Detective Stafford said he would be right down. You can wait over there if you like." He pointed to several chairs that were lined up next to one another by the far wall.

"If it's all the same to you, I'll wait right here," Ruby told the sergeant, afraid she might miss connecting with the detective if she was anywhere else in the police station. There was a great deal of activity going on in the area.

Because she wanted to be sure that all her *t*'s were crossed and her *i*'s dotted so that nothing would get in the way of her being able to adopt Maya, January had come with Sean to the police station. She gave her statement about what had taken place at the safe house and then signed all the necessary documents. She wanted no oversights or holdups getting in her way when the time came.

The adoption was beginning to look more and more like a real possibility. She and Sean had been up half the night, discussing the matter. They had come to the mutual agreement that the best thing for the little girl would be if they got married so that the adoption could go off without a problem.

January knew that, in Sean's case, getting married was just a means to a desired end—being able to adopt Maya. But she wasn't going to dwell on that.

"So, in essence, this is going to be a marriage of convenience," January had teased Sean in order to hide her insecurity.

"Trust me, convenience has absolutely nothing to do with you." The detective had laughed just before he took her into his arms.

Sean had merely intended to continue holding January until she fell asleep. But, inevitably, they wound up making love.

January had woken up this morning with a whole new frame of mind, ready to take on the world and make everything in it right.

They had gone together to see Maya. January then went through the draining task of telling the little girl that her father was gone, and he wasn't going to be coming back.

It took a long time for Maya to calm down and stop crying. But like the little trouper she had blossomed into, by the time they left her with Carly, Maya had started to come around.

* * *

After January gave her statement at the police station, she slowly regained her normal hopeful attitude. The adoption, no matter how it came about, was going to be a good thing for all of them, she thought—and then the desk sergeant had called, telling Sean that Maya's mother was down there, asking for her.

"Is the desk sergeant sure this woman is Maya's mother?" January asked, fearing the worst. "Because you know how these groupies have a tendency to come out of the woodwork, wanting to elbow their way into the limelight with some sort of made-up story."

And then, worried, January fell silent. If this woman really *was* Maya's mother, then the idea of adopting the little girl was beginning to seem like less of an option.

"We'll go down and talk to her to find out one way or another if she's on the level," Sean told her.

Sensing that January desperately needed support, Sean took her hand and squeezed it as they headed to the elevator.

"But if she *is* Maya's mother, how could she have put up with being separated from her child?" January asked angrily. There was no way she would have gone along with that if Maya had been hers.

"Maybe she had no choice," Sean suggested. "You saw what Mercer was like. That guy was pretty damn intimidating. He could have threatened Maya's mother— or both of them. And he had the backup thugs to do it."

January shot Sean a disgruntled look. "I hate it when you're being rational."

"I'll work on it," he promised, killing the smile that rose to his lips.

The moment they stepped off the elevator, January immediately spotted Ruby in front of the sergeant's desk. There was no wondering if she was the girl's mother.

January groaned. "Oh lord, she looks like a grown version of Maya."

Sean was looking at the woman, as well. "You see it, too," he noted. "I thought maybe it was just me."

Having heard the elevator's bell announce its arrival, Ruby looked over in that direction. Seeing the police detective coming toward her, she lost no time in striding over to him. She wound up meeting him and the woman accompanying him halfway.

"Is she here?" Ruby asked anxiously. Desperately wanting an answer and beside herself with worry, she had no time for formalities. "Is my baby here? She's not hurt, is she?"

"No, she's not hurt," Sean assured her. "But she's not here, either."

Ruby grew progressively more distressed. "Then where is she?" she demanded, looking from the detective to the woman with him.

It was January who spoke up. Considering the situation, her voice was deliberately calm, belying her own inner turmoil as she reassured Maya's mother. "She's with my two sisters and my cousin, a pediatric nurse— and she's very safe."

Ruby looked bewildered. Was this another detective? "Who are you?"

"I'm Maya's social worker," January explained, then introduced herself. "January Colton. And you are?"

Ruby drew herself up, knowing that her appearance probably left something to be desired. But she had come rushing over in her cashier's uniform the moment she heard the breaking news.

"My name is Ruby Duarte. Maya Duarte is my daughter." The last words came out in an almost stifled sob.

"Duarte, not Mercer?" Sean asked. Given the situation, that probably meant the cartel chieftain hadn't married the woman. He needed to delve deeper into the background story, Sean thought.

"Elias didn't want me to have any claim to our daughter, but given his line of work, he wanted to keep his options open just in case having a daughter wound up being a threat to his business dealings somewhere down the line." There were tears shimmering in the woman's brown eyes as she told him.

January read between the lines. There was no mistaking the animosity that existed between Ruby and her daughter's late father.

Ruby suddenly took January's hand. January sensed that Maya's mother thought the close contact would keep her from lying. She saw desperation in Ruby's tear-filled eyes.

"Where is Maya?" she asked again. "Can you take me to her?"

"How long has it been since you've seen her?" Sean asked.

"Officially, not since she was a baby and Elias took her away from me," Ruby answered.

The way she had phrased her reply begged another question. "And unofficially?" January asked.

"I have a picture of Maya that was taken five months ago. I have a friend who managed to find out where Maya was going to be one day. He covertly snapped this photograph for me." Ruby took out her phone and showed them the picture. She smiled ruefully as she told them, "I keep it next to me on my nightstand."

Looking at it with January, Sean nodded as he handed the phone back to Ruby. "I just need to substantiate a few things and then we can take you to see your daughter," he told the woman.

Ruby pressed her lips together as she nodded. January saw Maya's mother fighting back tears again. Tears that matched the ones she felt in her soul, January thought as she contemplated losing the child she had never really had.

The next hour, right after Ruby Duarte's story had been verified, was probably the hardest hour January had ever had to go through.

When she, Sean and Ruby finally arrived at the town house where her sisters and cousin were waiting with Maya, January could feel her heart breaking into little pieces. If this wound up going as well as she thought it would, January knew she was going to be saying goodbye to a little girl she had taken into her heart in an incredibly short amount of time.

Who would have ever thought that a bond between

her and the frightened little girl could have formed so quickly? January couldn't help marveling. She had come to care for a great many children in her line of work, but never to this extent.

But there was no denying that, right from the beginning, she had wanted nothing but the best for Maya. And the best was uniting the little girl with her mother.

A mother who obviously loved Maya a great deal.

When she and Sean walked in, Maya greeted them both with unabashed delight, hugging first one, then the other and then beginning the process all over again.

"Boy, she certainly did seem to miss you two," Simone observed.

"The entire time you were gone, she was totally antsy," Tatum told them. "Like she was afraid you wouldn't be coming back."

All three women in the room looked at the stranger who had come in with January and Sean.

"January, who's this?" Simone asked, taking the lead and looking at Ruby.

"This is Maya's mother," January answered, her voice completely devoid of any emotion for the moment.

The pain of letting go was almost too much to bear, but for Maya's sake, January knew she had to do it. This wasn't about her or what she wanted, this was about Maya and what was best for the little girl.

Maya was watching January as if she somehow sensed that this person who had come in with her and Sean was someone special. Turning, Maya signed the question to January.

As she started to reply, she was surprised to see Ruby

taking over. Signing to Maya, Ruby introduced herself to her daughter.

Maya looked by turns stunned, then hesitant and finally, a very shy smile came to her lips. She obviously had no memory of her mother, but she appeared very willing to finally have a real mother in her life.

"You know how to sign," January heard herself saying to Ruby. For some reason, she hadn't thought that Ruby would know how.

"The moment I discovered that my baby couldn't hear, I started learning how to communicate with her. Even when Elias took her from me and threatened me with dire consequences if I ever tried to reconnect with her, I just continued learning, hoping that she and I would someday be together again. I never gave up hope," Ruby said with feeling, signing the sentiment as she said it. "Never."

January took a deep breath. "Well, looks like you were right," she said. Ignoring how she felt inside, January forced herself to put on a positive face for Maya's sake.

Doing her best to rally, she told Maya's mother, "I bought some things for her. Let me go and pack them for you."

January was trying her best to leave the room with some shred of dignity before she broke down altogether and cried.

"That would be very nice of you," Ruby replied gratefully. And then, pausing, she looked from January to Sean. "Could I talk to the two of you for a minute before we leave?"

"Of course," Sean agreed. He gestured over to the side, but not before asking January's relatives for a favor. "You won't mind staying with Maya a little longer, right?"

"You take as long as you like," Simone said encouragingly, speaking for all three of them. She waved the detective and her sister off.

"What did you want to say to us?" January asked Maya's mother the moment they had all stepped aside.

Ruby appeared a little uneasy as she began to speak. "I couldn't help noticing that Maya seems to have formed a real bond with both of you. She clearly trusts you and I can see that she's very fond of both you and the detective."

January exchanged looks with Sean. "Yes," she agreed. "Your daughter's a very bright, sweet little girl."

Sean handed Maya's mother his business card. "If you need anything at all, I can be reached at this number day or night."

Ruby looked at the card before pocketing it. "Well, as it happens," she told them, "I think I am going to have to impose on you."

January was instantly alert. Was this going to be good or bad? "Oh?"

"Since you both seem to have formed a bond with my daughter, I was wondering if you would mind very much helping me with what is going to be the difficult transition of becoming Maya's mother again. I know I have no right to ask after everything you have already done, but I thought, since it's obvious that she likes you both so much, it would be easier for her to have you—"

"Say no more," January cried. "I'd love to help you and Maya reconnect."

"*We* would love to help you and Maya reconnect," Sean corrected, giving January a look that told her he intended to be in on this, as well.

Ruby looked completely relieved. "I can't thank you both enough for going out of your way like this and helping out," Ruby told them with overwhelming sincerity.

"No need to thank us. Just seeing Maya smile like that," January said, gesturing toward the little girl, "is more than enough for me."

"For us," Sean corrected her.

January nodded as she smiled. She was finally starting to relax.

This could turn out well, after all, she thought as she echoed Sean's words. "For us."

Chapter 23

It was several days later before a routine began to form and fall into place. Things finally settled down.

Much to Ruby Duarte's relief and joy, with January and Sean's help, she was able to step back into Maya's life. With what turned out to be a minimum of effort, the woman reclaimed her rightful place as the little girl's mother.

"I will always, always be grateful to both of you," Ruby told January and Sean. "I want you to feel free to come by any time. You'll always be welcome here."

"Just don't forget to invite us to your graduation ceremony," January told Maya's mother, referring to the nursing degree that Ruby was earning.

"Count on it," Ruby promised, standing beside her

daughter in the brand-new apartment January had helped her find for herself and Maya.

"So," Sean commented as they drove away, "looks like everything is going well for Maya and her mom. Why don't we go out and celebrate?"

"You mean, like, on a date?" January asked. With all the time they had spent together protecting Maya and then making plans for her future, they had never actually been out on a date.

"Exactly like on a date. How about we have dinner at your sister's restaurant? I hear the food's great," he said with a grin.

"Sure," January replied, but there was no enthusiasm in her voice.

As they drove there, Sean found that he was doing most of the talking. If January responded at all, it was in one- or two-word answers.

Arriving at the restaurant, Sean parked his sedan, but remained seated, observing his companion. This didn't bode well for his plans for the evening, he thought.

"You're awfully quiet tonight," he noted. "Something wrong?"

January was just going to shrug off his concern, but then thought better of it. She wasn't in the habit of lying and she wasn't about to start now. Besides, she had discovered that Sean had a way of seeing through her, so there was no use in even pretending everything was all right.

She knew this would probably sound foolish since, technically, she had just seen the girl, but January still told him what was eating away at her.

"I miss Maya," January confessed. There was this painful, gaping hole in her heart. She knew exactly how Ruby must have felt when Kid had taken her daughter from her.

Sean surprised her with his response. He didn't make a comment about her overreacting. Instead, he told her, "So do I." Stunned, she stared at the police detective. "But you have to admit," he went on, "that Maya's better off with her mother."

January sighed. "Yes, I know," she reluctantly agreed, then tried to rally by focusing on another aspect of this little drama. "Well, at least this turned out well for you."

She had lost him. "How do you mean?" Sean asked.

"Well, with her mother coming forward to claim Maya," January explained, "you've got to admit that certainly lets you off the hook." Belatedly, she forced herself to smile at him, as if this outcome at least benefited Sean.

"Off the hook?" he repeated, amazed that January would even think of putting it that way. "Did it ever occur to you that I didn't want to be off the hook? If anything," Sean went on, "I wanted to be *on* the hook." Didn't she understand that? he couldn't help wondering.

Her eyebrows drew together. Sean was lying to her. He was trying to be kind, but he was lying, she concluded. "No, you didn't. With the exception of my dad and my uncle, no man I've ever met *wants* to be on the hook. Men prefer to be free, to come and go as they damn well please," January insisted, and Sean wasn't going to convince her otherwise.

"And this is coming from where?" the detective asked. "From your vast relationship experience?"

"All right," she conceded. So this wasn't firsthand experience on her part, but that didn't make her conclusion any less valid. "It's coming from observing people as a social worker. It comes from having woman after woman pour out their hearts to me because they believed the fabricated lies of some guy who promised to be there and love them forever, only to disappear the moment it had the air of becoming serious—or she became pregnant."

Sean nodded. Just as he'd thought. If tonight was going to turn out the way he hoped, he had to convince her that she was laboring under a misapprehension.

"If you ask me, you've been dealing with a deck that's only been stacked one way." He paused for a minute, looking at her. And then he made up his mind.

He was going to push ahead. His heart gave him no choice.

"This wasn't the way I wanted to do this," he told her. "But maybe I should."

It was her turn not to understand. "Maybe you should what?"

He could feel his heart beginning to accelerate as he continued. "I was going to ask you if you would consider making our living arrangement permanent."

His question didn't clear up anything for her. It just made things even more obscure. "You want to move in with me on a permanent basis?" she asked, attempting to make some kind of sense out of what Sean was telling her.

"No, I want you to marry me on a permanent basis." Watching her face, he asked, "What do you say?"

She was surprised when she actually found her tongue. "I—"

And that was when two members of her family suddenly descended on them.

"Hey, Jan, Sean," Carly cried, looking obviously delighted. "Tatum said you were having dinner here." January's cousin made herself at home, taking a seat.

"So, how have you been?" Simone asked, sitting on the other side of her cousin. If she and Carly realized they were interrupting something, they certainly weren't acting as if they were aware of it. "We were going to grab a bite to eat here ourselves, and then Tatum told us that you two were already here." She beamed at her sister and her police detective. "So here we are," she announced—as if that was actually necessary.

January dearly loved her entire family, but she couldn't help thinking that her sister and her cousin couldn't have come at a worse possible time. Sean had asked her a question—*the* question—and was obviously waiting for an answer.

January looked at the police detective apologetically. This was normal behavior as far as her family was concerned, with members from both sides thinking nothing of popping up out of the blue without any warning and just commingling. But she knew this wasn't something he was used to taking in stride. She regarded Sean ruefully.

"Before I answer your question," January said to him, "how do you feel about being part of a crazy family like this? Because this—" she circled the general area that included her sister and her cousin with her hand "—isn't unusual. This is actually part of the norm."

January watched his face intently for some indication that the man was debating heading for the hills for his own self-preservation.

"How do *I* feel about being part of it?" Sean echoed.

January nodded. "That's the question."

Sean's couldn't have smiled any wider if he had tried. "I feel great about it," he told her with unabashed enthusiasm.

Simone exchanged looks with her sister and then stared at the detective. "What are you two talking about? *What* about our crazy family?" Simone asked.

Sean had just given her his answer, so she was just about to give him hers—and it was a positive one.

"Well, if you must know," January began, "Sean and I have just decided—"

Sean's cell phone went off just then, interrupting what January had been about to share. "Hold that thought," he requested, looking down at his cell phone's screen. "I've got to take this call. It's from my lieutenant."

Maybe it had to do with something more about the dead cartel chieftain, he thought.

Rising from the table, Sean stepped away to give Walters his full attention. He knew that if he remained sitting where he was, he wouldn't be able to concentrate on what his lieutenant had to say. Not under the present circumstances.

The moment Sean walked away from the table, Simone looked at her sister. "So, give," she ordered. "Did he just ask you to marry him?"

Carly was only half a beat behind Simone. "More importantly, did you say yes?"

Oh no, she wasn't about to do this on her own. In her mind, she and Sean were already a couple. "You heard Sean. He wants to be here before anything's said," January told the other two women.

Simone pretended to ignore her sister and turned toward their cousin. "Look at that face," she said, nodding toward January. "She's grinning from ear to ear. She said yes," the oldest Colton sister said confidently. Then she glanced at January. "You did say yes, didn't you?"

January shook her head. "I told you, Simone, it's not exclusively my story to tell."

"C'mon, Jan, don't be that way. We've been through so many things together. You can't just pick now to shut us out," Carly complained.

Simone looked up to see the man she assumed was going to be her future brother-in-law heading back to their table.

"Ah, speak of the devil," she said, winking at Sean as he drew close. "We were just trying to get your partner in crime to spill the beans and tell us what's going on."

In light of the expression she saw on the detective's face, Simone dropped her teasing tone. "Sean?" she asked seriously. "Is something wrong?"

He looked at the three women seated at the table, wondering how he was going to break what had to be the worst possible news they would ever hear.

For that matter, how was he going to find the words to tell January?

Something had frozen within him the second he had heard the news himself, and now he had to be the one to say those crushing words out loud to January and her sister and cousin.

And once the words were out, Sean knew he couldn't unsay them, couldn't find a way to take back the pain they would create.

But whether or not he could take them back didn't change the fact that it had happened.

And they needed to know.

"Sean," January said in a very still voice. "What is it? You're scaring me. Who was that just now on the phone?"

He was just making this worse, Sean thought. His not saying anything just deepened the tension, the horror of the situation that had just come to pass.

"That was my lieutenant," Sean told her. Each word he uttered felt as if it weighed a ton as it came out of his mouth.

"And?" Carly pressed, growing as uneasy as her cousins.

"For heaven sakes, Sean, it can't be *that* bad," Simone insisted. "Just what did this lieutenant of yours say?"

In the course of his career, he had been the bearer of this kind of awful news a number of times. It was something he had never gotten used to. But in all that time, the news had never been a personal matter.

It was today.

"I was just informed of a double homicide," he heard himself telling the women.

"A double homicide," Carly repeated, as if repeating the words would make her able to absorb the news better. And understand it.

"Who were the victims?" Simone asked, her voice suddenly stony, removed.

He felt January reach for his hand, wrapping her fingers around it in an attempt to brace herself.

Sean squeezed her hand before uttering the words no one wanted to hear. He would have been willing to give up his own life to spare her and her family this anguish and grief.

"Ernest and Alfred Colton. Your father and uncle," he added numbly before saying, "They were gunned down tonight as they left their office."

He was aware of January trying to muffle the anguished sob that rose to her lips.

She failed.

Taking her into his arms, Sean made her and the other two women a promise right then and there. "I'm not going to rest until I find out who did this to your father and uncle—and why."

And he would love January forever and help in the darkest times. Times like this one, where the world seemed to be falling apart for the Colton family.

No one said a word. They all too busy dealing with the overwhelming, gut-wrenching pain and grief generated by this sudden crime that had come out of nowhere.

One question invaded and dominated all of their minds: Why?

* * * * *

Don't miss the next exciting romance in the
Colton 911: Chicago miniseries:
Colton 911: Unlikely Alibi *by Lisa Childs,*
available next month from
Harlequin Romantic Suspense.

COMING NEXT MONTH FROM

H HARLEQUIN

ROMANTIC SUSPENSE

Available February 9, 2021

#2123 COLTON 911: UNLIKELY ALIBI
Colton 911: Chicago • by Lisa Childs
Kylie Givens has been Heath Colton's right hand ever since she joined his family's company, but when he's accused of murder in order to take over the business, she becomes his false alibi. As the real killer threatens them both, they're forced into very close quarters.

#2124 COLTON'S KILLER PURSUIT
The Coltons of Grave Gulch • by Tara Taylor Quinn
First Everleigh Emerson was framed for murder, then someone tried to kill her—twice. But the real threat comes when she falls for the man who exonerated her, PI Clarke Colton. Only time will tell if she emerges unscathed...or more endangered than ever.

#2125 HUNTED IN CONARD COUNTY
Conard County: The Next Generation
by Rachel Lee
Kerri Addison, a disabled former cop now teaching criminal law, teams up with Officer Stuart Canady to hunt a rapist who is stalking women in Conard County, Wyoming. But can Kerri let Stuart close enough to her before the perpetrator ends them—permanently?

#2126 RANGER'S FAMILY IN DANGER
Rangers of Big Bend • by Lara Lacombe
One night of passion results in a pregnancy, but Sophia doesn't tell Carter he's going to be a dad right away. Now she's back in town with his son, and someone is threatening them. Can he keep the woman he loves and his baby safe, despite his broken heart?

YOU CAN FIND MORE INFORMATION ON UPCOMING HARLEQUIN TITLES,
FREE EXCERPTS AND MORE AT HARLEQUIN.COM.

HRSCNM0121

SPECIAL EXCERPT FROM

HHARLEQUIN
ROMANTIC SUSPENSE

*One night of passion results in a pregnancy, but Sophia
doesn't tell Carter he's going to be a dad right away.
Now she's back in town with his son, and someone is
threatening them. Can he keep the woman he loves and
his baby safe, despite his broken heart?*

*Read on for a sneak preview of
Ranger's Family in Danger,
the next thrilling romance in the
Rangers of Big Bend miniseries
by Lara Lacombe.*

She shivered next to him, clearly upset as she spoke. He
put his arm around her and pressed a kiss to the top of
her head.

"It's okay," he soothed, stroking her upper arm. "I'm
here now. I won't let anyone hurt you or Ben."

"I think he has a key."

That got his attention. He paused midstroke, digesting
this bit of news. "What makes you say that?"

She told him about Jake Porter, the man who claimed
to be Will's grandson. The way he'd visited her earlier,
his displeasure at finding her in the house.

"We'll change all the locks," Carter declared. "I'll go
first thing in the morning, as soon as the hardware stores
open. We can even put some extra locks on, as additional
deterrent. And I want you and Ben to stay with me until

he's apprehended." His apartment wasn't large, but they would make it work. She could have his bed and he'd take the couch. The discomfort was a small price to pay for knowing she and the baby were safe.

"Oh, no," she said. "We can't do that."

Carter drew back and stared at her, blinking in confusion. This was a no-brainer. Someone was out there with an agenda, and it was clear they were after something inside this house. Changing the locks was a good first step, but he doubted the intruder was going to be put off so easily. Unless he missed his guess, this guy was going to come back. And the next time, he might not be content to simply ransack a few rooms.

Carter took her hand. "I'm not trying to be alarmist here, but he's probably going to try again."

"But the locks," she said weakly.

"I doubt he'll let new locks stop him," Carter replied. "And given the way he acted with you before, it's probably only going to escalate. If he finds you here, he might hurt you."

Don't miss
Ranger's Family in Danger *by Lara Lacombe,*
available February 2021 wherever
Harlequin Romantic Suspense
books and ebooks are sold.

Harlequin.com